The party was over for Vivian

Her Long Island mansion was filled with guests, but Vivian left them when a maid said her brother was at the gate. As she reached it, two men suddenly emerged from hiding and strong arms grasped her.

Terrified and panic-stricken, she struggled against her captors, but to no avail. When she opened her mouth to scream, a cloth reeking with chloroform was clamped over her face.

As she breathed the fumes, she sank into a swirling black pool, the words *Why? Why?* pounding in her ears.

Other

MYSTIQUE BOOKS

by MAGALI

 1 VANISHING BRIDE
 7 THE MASTER OF PALOMAR
10 IN SEARCH OF SYBIL
20 THE MOMENT OF TRUTH
24 LOSS OF INNOCENCE
56 NIGHT OF THE STORM

For a free catalogue listing all available Mystique Books,
send your name and address to:

MYSTIQUE BOOKS,
M.P.O. Box 707, Niagara Falls, N.Y. 14302
In Canada: 649 Ontario St., Stratford, Ontario N5A 6W2

Captive in Paradise

by MAGALI

MYSTIQUE BOOKS

TORONTO • LONDON • NEW YORK
HAMBURG • AMSTERDAM

CAPTIVE IN PARADISE/first published February 1980

ISBN 0-373-50068-8

PRINTED IN U.S.A.

Chapter 1

It was a day of great festivity; my husband and I were entertaining just about everyone who was anyone in the New York publishing and entertainment communities. *World News*, the magazine originated by my husband, Martin Fawkes—and which, by the way, he continues to run with ever increasing success—was having its twelfth anniversary.

Celebrities of all kinds had been invited, as well as the lesser-known but influential owners of the largest financial institutions, not to mention a generous sprinkling of political dignitaries and titled gentry. Naturally, with such a gathering of newsworthy personalities, representatives of the press would be everywhere. Our house, a nineteenth-century mansion on Long Island, had been recently decorated with exquisite taste by a very fashionable New York designer. A canopy was erected to protect the entire length of the walk from the entrance gates to the front door of the house.

In all, more than four hundred people had been invited,
too many to be accommodated in comfort in our house,
large as it was. Tents, beautifully decorated with a profusion of potted plants and cut flowers, had been set up in
the courtyard to take care of the overflow. The unusually
balmy fall evening felt like the last day of summer. The
abundant flowers created a delirious splash of color
against the already splendid autumn blooms.

An army of waiters was hired to serve the three buffets
set out in readiness for our guests. A steel band was set up
in the side garden. That, together with a disco room for the
downtown crowd and a chamber orchestra for the more
sedate group, ensured a lively evening of varied entertainment. Numerous small tables, their snow white cloths of
fine linen sparkling with place settings of silver and crystal,
a specially arranged bouquet of fresh tropical flowers set in
the center of each, awaited the guests. A tropical theme,
clever lighting and a variety of the finest wines and liquors
completed the preparations for one of the most important
events of the year in New York society.

As each famous name was announced from the top of
the stairs, Martin and I greeted the new arrival on the terrace. Then they were directed to their tables by hostesses in
bright floral prints, especially designed for this occasion by
Elton, a young and innovative American designer who was
currently enjoying a favorable reputation in Europe.

It wasn't long before the guest list began to seem never-
ending, even though the evening had just begun. My legs
were aching and my feet were telling me with more and
more insistence that my shoes were very new. It was becoming quite an effort to keep my smile spontaneous as I
continued to greet each new arrival.

Much to my continual amazement, invitations to our

parties were highly regarded and coveted in the "in" social circles in New York. An invitation to this reception had become a very definite status symbol. Not having been born into so-called society, I was still, after several years of marriage, in awe of the world I found myself in. Was this real? Was this really *me* greeting these prestigious people?

My husband's social position was at the top of the heap—and he intended to keep it that way. Perhaps more than anything else—more than his houses, his race horses, his boats—he valued his position in society. If anything, his wealth and his possessions simply served as his ticket into high society. Once in, his charm, his spirit and his reputation as an honorable man, at least as one who avoided the more murky aspects of human dealings, ensured his popularity within the innermost circles.

I was well aware of my husband's fame as an excellent host and man of the world. Strong-willed and authoritative, he believed in taking life in very large bites. A fine figure of a man, he was definitely attractive, even more so at forty-four than he had been at thirty-seven. There was sixteen years' age difference between us, just enough to flatter his masculinity for having a young wife without being accused of being a "dirty old man"—for goodness knows, he wouldn't have wanted any scandal. He had a seasoned dignity, assurance and sensuality about him that women gravitated toward. We had been married for seven years. From time to time I stole a glance at him as he kissed the proffered hand of each woman as though she were specially singled out. He was like a royal prince, bestowing his favors upon his humble subjects.

Finally, there was a lull in the stream of new arrivals. Martin seemed to be angry with me, which wasn't all that unusual. His look was definitely one of discontent.

"Why didn't you wear your emeralds, Vivian?" he asked
dryly.

Here we go again, I thought to myself. Involuntarily,
my hand sought my neckline. "I thought that my
pearls. . . ."

"You thought wrong," he interrupted, his voice bitter.
"Look around you. Is anyone wearing pearls this year?
The emeralds would have been perfect with that green
dress. I paid a fortune for those emeralds and I don't want
them left in a jewel case gathering dust."

Suddenly he stopped talking and the expression on his
face changed. Instantly he was all charm as a new name
was called from the stairs and a couple approached. I
sighed with relief. The moment had been saved by the new
arrivals.

An hour passed and my role as hostess in the reception
line finally came to an end. Quietly I moved away from
Martin and began to mingle with the guests, pretending to
check on a few details to make sure that everything was
running smoothly.

Inside the house the party was in full swing—the joyful
mingling of the crowd bordered on chaos. Groups were
formed as old friends met, each group growing larger and
larger by the minute.

People were coming and going in a continuous stream,
pushing and shoving. Absolute strangers, determined to be
noticed, reached out to stop me as I passed by. I was
congratulated on the decor, the food, the house, my
dress . . . compliments seemed to be coming from
everywhere, each more outrageous than the last.

I played right along, sometimes laughing, sometimes
looking down with false modesty and at all times attempting to appear unconcerned. The men seemed sincere

enough, but I was sure I could see a certain reticence in the women's eyes. Clearly, they were envious. Yes, I was a very lucky woman. Yes, my husband undoubtedly was an extraordinary man. Who would know better than I?

I was the young wife of Martin Fawkes, tycoon, who had been nice enough to notice me when I was merely twenty-one. He was, as everyone was bold enough to point out at the time, quite a catch. Rich, handsome, charming—what could be more desirable in life than to be the wife of Martin Fawkes?

Meanwhile, my feet hurt. It seemed that it really didn't matter how many hundreds of dollars one spent on slender leather thongs strapped to heels—when they hurt, they hurt. I wanted nothing more than to get away from all these strangers who claimed to be friends and to find a nice quiet corner where I could sit down in peace.

Gradually I worked myself through the crowd and made my way to the back of the house and out into the garden. There were several tents set up in the back, as well as tables, but the scene was a quieter one, interrupted only by the sounds coming from the steel band at the side of the house. Quite a few people gathered around the buffet table and surrounding tents. I headed for the tent at the far end of the garden, which had been reached by only a few people. The tables were empty and the bar deserted. I walked to the bar and asked for a Manhattan. As I waited for the bartender to mix it, I furtively kicked off my shoes and hopped from one foot to the other.

I recoiled in surprise at the touch of a hand on my bare shoulder.

"What's the matter? Is there something wrong with your feet?"

I slumped in relief. It was Sandra Milanoff, the one person in the world I could feel happy about seeing at that moment.

I pointed to the green sandals that matched my dress.

"You should have bought a larger size," she exclaimed in her raucous voice. Sandra had a voice and laugh that would have sounded crass coming from anyone else. In her case, they were part of her charm.

Sandra and I had been good friends since we had won the Tennis Cup together. The competition was supposed to be confined to members of the press, but I had been allowed to enter because I was the publisher's wife. At the time, Martin was attempting to educate me, make me a woman of the world. . .a bona fide member of New York society.

Sandra looked at me and laughed. As usual, she looked quite stunning, albeit slightly eccentric. She was wearing a black ensemble that clung to her body, accentuating her flaming red hair. "What are you drinking?" she asked as the bartender handed me my glass.

"A Manhattan. Would you like one?"

"Not me," she said. "Make mine a vodka. . .a double."

We walked to the most remote corner of the bar and sat down on the bar stools. I picked up my shoes and held them in my lap.

"Am I late?" asked Sandra. "Did the boss say anything?"

"It doesn't matter," I replied. Lots of people will be dribbling in late. And anyway, you're not here by some kind of royal command, you know."

"That's what you think." She swirled the vodka in her glass with the tip of a finger. "I've been ordered by your tyrant of a husband to write up this wingding for my column in the paper. I should have been ahead of everyone else. Fortunately, the boss didn't see me come in. He was busy talking to Lady Guidoni."

It was Sandra's job to write the society column in Martin's newspaper, one of his many holdings both locally and internationally. She had little love or respect for most of the people she had to write about and seized every opportunity to take a verbal swipe at them.

"Seems to be quite a success, this party of the boss's," she said. "Whose idea was the tropical setting—yours?"

"No, it was the caterer's idea. You know how I am. . . ."

"Yes, you merely see that everything is done to perfection. Have you seen how everyone is taking all this in? You've certainly pulled it off this time!" Then she proffered a package of cigarettes. "Have one," she said.

"No, thanks. I don't smoke. You know that."

"You haven't got any vices, have you? Not even the usual minor ones," she sighed between puffs on her cigarette.

It almost seemed as though she resented my appearing not to have any faults. As I looked out the open doorway of the tent, I could see the multicolored lights on the trees. One particularly large tree stood by itself, as though in some kind of fairyland, stylized under the somber sky. It was October, the most beautiful time of year for the garden. Beautiful, but at the same time melancholy . . . like a dream that was being threatened.

People had started to invade our refuge. Sandra sipped on her vodka and murmured names to me as people she knew came through the doorway. She took a small note pad from her purse and balanced it on her knee to make notes.

I rested my sore feet on the base of the stool and daydreamed. The bartender put a fresh Manhattan on the bar in front of me and I didn't protest. After all, why shouldn't I get a little high?

I looked around the tent, taking in the comings and go-ings of the horde of people who filled our shelter. Sudden-ly, someone caught my attention. At the opposite end of the tent near the entrance, a tall figure had appeared. In the midst of all those people rushing around trying to find a place to sit, he stood quite motionless, like a rock in the middle of a stormy sea. Taller than most, he stood looking down at the crowd. He appeared to be looking for some-one in particular.

Eventually, Sandra noticed him. "Who's that?" she mur-mured, staring at him.

"I don't know. One of my husband's guests, no doubt."

He was wearing a white dinner jacket that made his handsome tanned face and thick, jet black hair stand out all the more. He was lean, yet muscular; there was something powerful in the slow, controlled manner of his move-ments. He had the grace and the wild, steady gaze of a cat. But there was also something about him that made me jumpy.

"Now, that's what I call divine!" said Sandra in a voice that might have been heard halfway across the room. "I've simply got to speak to him. I think I'll try for an interview. Catch you later."

She slipped down from the bar stool and hurried toward her victim. But before she could reach him, he looked directly at me with still, ice blue eyes, turned around and walked out of the tent. For reasons I couldn't explain, my heart stopped for a moment and I felt faint.

Sandra pressed forward in her attempt to catch up to him. People she knew kept stopping her along the way, and others rushing back and forth from their tables to the bar impeded her progress. Many of her colleagues were there and she did everything she could to keep the greetings short and her goal in sight.

I watched until she disappeared through the doorway. There was no way she was going to be able to catch up with this mysterious stranger and I was secretly glad, although I couldn't imagine why. Was I jealous and afraid that Sandra would beguile him with her charms? Or was I frightened and worried for her safety? Either way, I was taken aback. In a brief moment so much had happened. I felt weak with emotions I could not justify, much less explain.

Chapter 2

I decided to go back to the large dining room to preside at the table where the cultural attaché from France and other dignitaries had been seated. There, at least, I might slip my shoes off under the cover of the long, draped tablecloth. Also, I thought that the simple chitchat required of me would be restful. After so much work preparing for the party, I felt I deserved a rest—both from my duties as hostess and from my disturbing emotions and thoughts.

Two hours later I saw Sandra dancing gaily with one of the black correspondents from Africa. She winked at me as she whirled past, and later came back to join me at the table. My companions had left the table to go out to the garden and admire the lights.

"Aren't you dancing?" she asked.

"Are you kidding?" I replied. "In these shoes!" My feet were still killing me.

"You should take them off," she said. "Loosen the party up a bit."

She looked around the room and sighed. "Your husband seems to be spending a lot of time with the Italian ambassador's wife and the beautiful Sylvia Gaylord," she murmured significantly.

"She's his latest," I muttered.

"The ambassador's wife?"

"You're joking, of course," I said gruffly. The ambassador's wife was over sixty years old. "You know I mean the actress."

"I'm sorry. I shouldn't make jokes to you about this. But you know the boss. It doesn't mean anything."

"What makes you say that?"

Although Martin's affairs had always been a matter of acceptable public interest, Sandra and I had never talked openly about them. I was interested to find out how she saw things, and what she thought about the situation.

"He likes them all, doesn't he," she observed, turning a question into a statement of fact. "And none of them last very long."

There was a sadness in her usually jovial gruff voice. I looked at her, suspecting that in the past she, too, might very well have been one of the women Martin had found pleasing. Quite certain that it must have been before my time, though, I gave it no more than a passing thought.

"I'm sure I'm not telling you anything new," said Sandra.

I gave her a weary smile, feeling almost indifferent. Well, I had become indifferent over the years.

I decided that the time had come for me to tell Sandra what was on my mind. Several months earlier I had thought of confiding in her, of coming to her for advice. But I realized then that whatever my decision was going to be, I was the one who was going to have to live with it, so I was better off thinking it through on my own. Now I had given it sufficient thought and had made my decision. Sandra was my closest friend, and I knew that I should fill her in.

"Sandra," I ventured. I put my hand on her wrist. "There's something I want to tell you."

She dropped her cigarette into the ashtray. "Yes?" she asked. Her eyes registered surprise. She was obviously quite intrigued by my attitude. "You're so serious tonight!" she exclaimed, hoping to get our conversation on a more cheerful level.

"I want to talk to you about something. Can you keep a secret? And, particularly, this is something I wouldn't want to see in your column."

"Of course I can keep a secret. And believe me, I know precisely when not to be a journalist. Especially where a friend is concerned . . . and you are my friend."

It was true. I couldn't remember having had a better friend than Sandra.

"Well, here it is: I'm leaving."

Sandra's mouth dropped open. "Leaving? Where are you going?"

I simply moved my hand in a vague gesture. "Somewhere. Anywhere . . . ."

She looked at me for a few seconds without saying a word. We seemed to be sitting in a small pocket of silence in the middle of the world of noise coming from the living room and garden. I was glad to notice that there were few people near us. Even when Sandra whispered, her voice was quite loud and tended to carry. And this was one conversation I didn't want people overhearing.

"Are you serious?" asked Sandra finally in her very softest, most conspiratorial whisper, glancing around the room furtively.

"Absolutely!"

"Do you mean to tell me that you're going to leave this house?"

I motioned to her to lower her voice. Some people had come into the room and were milling around looking for a place to settle down.

"And Martin," I replied in a voice that was quite weary, but nonetheless definite. "I'm going to leave him...leave everything. I'm going to get away from this house, from Martin. To him, I'm really not much more than another piece of furniture. I'm just one more possession, like his yacht or his car. Well, I'm not a possession and I've had enough of being treated like one."

I stopped, trying to control my emotions before I went on. "I've had it up to here, Sandra. I'm tired of crying, being sick to my stomach.... Can't you understand how I feel?"

She seemed unable to convince herself that I was being serious and looked completely bewildered. "But I always thought that you and Martin got along fairly well—compared to most married couples, in any case. You never have fights and—"

"Of course we never have fights. We never talk! And when we do argue, Martin makes sure no one knows."

"What has Martin had to say about all this?"

"He doesn't know," I replied in a lower voice.

"I see.... You haven't told him yet." She sighed and sat up straight in her chair. Somehow, she seemed reassured. Perhaps she was thinking I was simply telling her these things in a moment of anger and would get over it.

She took a cigarette from the small silver dish on the

table and lit it before speaking. "Come now," she said finally. "I can't believe you're serious about all this. You should have a talk with him. Try to work it out. You just can't pack up and leave at the drop of a hat."

"What you're really saying is that I can't just walk out on this wealth, not Martin," I said sourly.

"Vivian, please don't get cross. I'm only trying to be constructive. I know I'm the last person you would expect to hear this from, but what I'm trying to say is that I think you have a responsibility to try to work things out."

"Do you think that Martin would ever give up seeing other women?"

"Well...no, but...."

"There. You see, there's no point in trying to work something out. He won't change. You know that and I know that. And I'm just not the type of woman that can be happy in this situation, even with all the expensive goodies. Call me old-fashioned, but I think that a husband and wife should be faithful and should love each other. I can't live with this empty shell of a relationship that means nothing to—"

"You're serious, then?" Sandra interrupted, cutting off my explanation. I think it pained Sandra to hear the truth of my feelings about my marriage.

Sandra was still single, and she liked to believe in happily-ever-after fairy tales, hoping that she, too, would meet Prince Charming and go to live in his castle. I think it upset her to hear the bleak reality, much as she might have been suspecting it all along.

"You're going to have to believe it, Sandra. I'm more serious about this than I've ever been about anything in my life."

"But you do love each other...don't you? Even a little?"

"No."

No was such a short little word, and yet I found it one of the hardest to say. It hadn't been easy owning up to the fact that there was no love between Martin and myself. I guess I had fallen for the fairy-tale fantasy myself. I wanted so much to believe in our marriage, for it to work forever, but it had become impossible to hide from the fact that there was nothing between us.

It was quite obvious that Sandra was not at all touched by my conviction. When she spoke, it was in a conciliatory tone. "You're just tired," she murmured. "Mind you, in some ways I can certainly understand why you feel the way you do. A little bit of this kind of life can go a long way, and Martin does seem to get carried away. But...well, you know...."

I simply sat and stared at her for a minute. "You're wasting your time, Sandra," I said finally. "No matter what you might be thinking about saying, I've heard it all before. I've been talking to myself for some time now. Earlier, you said that my husband's affairs don't mean anything. Well, I know my position is supposed to be enviable, that I have all sorts of advantages and my life is some kind of bed of roses. The truth of the matter is that I hate my life. I simply can't take it any longer. Can't you understand?"

Despite my determination to remain calm, my voice had risen and I had become angry. It was Sandra's turn to quieten me. She discreetly gestured toward the people around us. I glanced around the room and was startled by a glimpse of the back of a tall man in a white jacket, slipping out the door at the rear of the room. Was it the man we had seen in the tent?

"You're just depressed tonight," Sandra continued, murmuring across the table. "You've been working so hard on this party—it's sure to be a big letdown. Things will look better in the morning, they always do."

What she was saying merely irritated me further. "I won't be here in the morning," I said.

Her eyes opened wide. "What?" Then she went on in a voice that seemed suddenly unsure. "When are you planning to leave?"

"In a few minutes."

This time, Sandra was definitely shocked. She looked quite bewildered and spoke to me as if she were addressing a child. "You're saying foolish things," she said. "Where will you go?"

"That's my business," I replied.

"All right. I'll drink to that," she laughed. Sandra had always said that she liked my spunk, and I suppose she thought I was being spunky now. Little did she know that I was simply being serious. But I must have been getting the message across somehow. As we sat in silence for a few moments, her face grew more and more tense.

"I really don't mean to pry," she said finally. "But you do have to live, you know. We all get fed up with things once in a while, but it isn't always wise to go to extremes in our reactions. Unfortunately, that's something we're inclined to do when we're hurt and upset. We rebel."

"This isn't a whim," I stated. "It's something I've been planning for a long time. I've thought it all out, and nothing is going to stop me from going through with it."

Sandra's voice became more vehement. "But, just think of what you're doing! You're being absolutely absurd! What's going to happen to you?" Suddenly she stopped as an idea struck her. Her eyebrows went up and she looked at me with a half smile. "Don't tell me you . . . ."

I simply shrugged. "Sorry to disappoint you, Sandra, but there isn't another man. No one else is involved at all. I've simply decided to get away from a life I can't take any longer. Life is nothing without joy and there's no joy for me here. I'm just a showpiece, always on parade. I'm expected to dress well, keep my hair nice, wear just the right amount of makeup and then...then appear! Do you understand what I'm saying? I appear at meetings and dinners and fancy-dress balls and receptions...but not as a real person. Oh, no, I'm not a person at all....

"Oh, Sandra, I've reached the point where I don't even know what I am! I tell you, I've got to get out! This is no way to live. You asked what was going to happen to me. Well, I've been asking myself the same thing and haven't come up with any answers. All I know is that there isn't any future for me here."

Sandra looked as if she didn't know what to say. She shrugged her shoulders awkwardly. "You have to admit, though, that you do enjoy certain compensations."

"Compensations? What can compensate for lost time, happiness that's been missed? I'm twenty-eight years old and I find I don't have any self-respect. I thought of myself as idealistic when I married Martin. Now I know that I was just foolish."

She made a vague gesture with her hand. "If you're going to talk about being idealistic...."

"I know," I replied. "It isn't exactly in fashion."

Suddenly I had had enough of the discussion. I was sick of talking about my unhappiness, sick of thinking about it. The time for all that had long since past. Now it was time for action. "Please excuse me, Sandra," I said. "I really must go."

She finally seemed to realize just what was happening and put a hand on my arm to stop me. "But, Vivian...have you thought about finances? Until now, Martin has provided everything you've needed. What are you going to do for money?"

"Don't worry, Sandra. I've thought of that, too. For one thing, I won't be needing very much. After all, I was happier before I got married to Martin, and I didn't have any money then. I can learn to do without the frills if I have to."

"Yes, but food and rent aren't frills. How will you live? I hate to be blunt, but you're a bit old for modeling, and what else could you do?"

It was true. And the facts did hurt. I had met Martin when I was twenty-one. I had just quit university for financial reasons and gone into high-fashion modeling on the advice of some friends. They assured me my tall, slender figure, high cheekbones, widely spaced, large green eyes and abundant black hair were all that was needed.

It astonished me how successful I was. I couldn't believe the way people were constantly fawning over me, as if I were some superstar. And all for the sake of how I looked; it had nothing to do with *me* at all. But I did make a lot of money at it, and at that time money was very important to my family.

My father had died when I was nineteen, and the provisions of his will left more debts than anything else. My mother, who was alive then, did what she could, but after a while it was too much for her. My brother was five years younger, still in school and living at home. I think it broke my mother's heart to have to ask me to quit university and find a job. The success had I enjoyed as a fashion model came as a pleasant surprise, although I was more than happy to give it all up when I married Martin.

Now, I knew, there was no way I could get back into it again. Even though I was still very slender, and sometimes passed for twenty-one, I was definitely over the hill as far as the fashion scene was concerned. The camera never lies about your real age. Another factor to contend with was that I would be starting from the bottom once more. It would take some time to develop modeling into a decent living. But I had already thought all of this out and had made other plans.

"I know I'm too old for modeling now," I said to Sandra, who seemed surprised that I wasn't crushed by what she had said. "And I wouldn't want to get back into it anyway, even though the money is good."

"Don't knock money, Vivian. Money is not that easy to come by, believe me," Sandra said, like the seasoned old newspaper veteran that she was.

"I'm not, but. . . ." I suddenly became aware that there was a man standing quietly at my elbow. How long had he been there? I stopped talking and looked up at him. It was Philippe, the headwaiter, who apologized for interrupting but explained that he was having trouble with a guest in the disco room on the second floor.

"What seems to be the problem, Philippe?" I asked in my best "I'm the Boss" voice. Even after seven years in that role, I found it a strain.

"It's Count Perrin, madam, and. . . ." The waiter looked uncomfortably toward Sandra, whose pen and pad of paper were lying among the table debris of empty glasses and full ashtrays.

"Go ahead. What's the problem?" I asked, at the same time giving Sandra a look that meant that she was not to regard any of what she heard as information for her column. Sheepishly she nodded her assent and looked the other way. Such tidbits of embarrassing gossip were what her readers counted on, and she hated not being able to use them.

"Well...it seems that he has had a bit too much, and...."

"You mean he's drunk?" Sandra exclaimed in her loud voice, causing several couples nearby to turn and stare.

"Evidently," Philippe answered, undaunted by Sandra's teasing. "He's undressing while doing a not-too-discreet dance that he calls the Hustle Hustle."

Sandra couldn't repress a laugh, and I had to admit that I was having a hard time of it myself. "Have you talked to Mr. Fawkes?" I asked Philippe.

"Yes. He asked not to be disturbed for any reason." Sandra and I exchanged wry, knowing looks.

"Well, find out what people the count came with," I said, "and if possible suggest to them that they press him into going home or staying clothed. But whatever you do, avoid embarrassing the count."

Philippe nodded his assent and turned to go. "And Philippe," I added before he was off and running, "see that someone cleans these tables. They're a mess."

After Philippe had gone, I turned to Sandra. "You know, one would think that I lead a life of leisure. If you only knew! Think of the staff it takes to run all the homes and boats, much less carry on all the entertaining. All my time is taken up with these petty details." I sighed wearily.

"You know," Sandra said with a laugh, "I never looked at it that way, but I see what you mean."

"Where were we, anyway?"

"Something about money—or the lack of it, to be more precise."

"Oh, right. Well, I've a plan. I'm not interested in being

a model again. Did I ever tell you that before I got married I was studying to be an occupational therapist? I even went back to school after we were married, but Martin didn't like the 'image,' he said, and I found it too hard to be in school and at the same time do all the things I was supposed to do as Martin's wife. So I quit. Well, now I'd like to go back to that. It's what I've always wanted to do. Actually, I'm quite excited about it."

Sandra looked at me in total bewilderment. She had always seen me as a carefree, happy creature, spending money freely and not giving much thought to things. Now, she was seeing the real me. She was shocked.

I told her a little of what I had been planning, explaining some of the things that I had done. I even mentioned that I had sold my jewels. "I realize, of course, that the jewels were just an investment to Martin. And as long as I wore them, they were also visible evidence of his fortune. But they were gifts to me, after all. And that money will help me set up a new home and finish my schooling."

Then I went on to describe some of the most recent steps I had taken. "I'm all packed," I said. "In fact, I took my suitcases to the depot this morning and put them in a locker. In a few minutes I'll call a taxi and quietly leave. With all the excitement going on around here, nobody will even notice. And I'll be in plenty of time to catch my bus. By the time they realize I'm gone, I'll be far away."

Sandra was dumbfounded. I had spoken with such calm that she was convinced I was telling the truth. Finally she was willing to accept that I wasn't bluffing. She got up from her chair and stood beside me, the expression on her face a mixture of excitement and concern.

Then she tried one final argument. "Have you thought about how this will affect Martin?"

"I know Martin won't like it. It will be a blow to his masculine pride, after all. But I'm sure he'll survive. I've written him a letter and I'll put it in his room. When he finds it later on, he'll think I've gone away for just a short while. We've been apart before, you know. I don't think he'll worry too much, in any event. His pride may be hurt a little, but it won't take him long to get over it."

Sandra nodded her head. "You seem to have thought of everything."

"Yes."

For a moment, neither of us spoke. Then, with a toss of her head, Sandra turned to look at me. "Well," she exclaimed. "This is quite something!" Her expression softened and her eyes grew tender. "Vivian," she added in a voice that had become quite shy. "Promise that you'll keep in touch with me?"

"I promise. You'll be hearing from me, I promise you."

A group of press reporters entered the room and descended on Sandra. They, like everyone else, had been caught up in the gay spirit of the party. "Come on!" they called out, pulling her to her feet.

"Good luck," she whispered to me, squeezing my hand as she was swept away. "And remember, keep in touch."

We went our separate ways, Sandra to be caught up in her group of peers and I to go upstairs for the last time. I made my way from room to room, smiling, acknowledging greetings from the hundreds of people dancing, eating, drinking. . . .

Everywhere I turned there was a crush of people. The garden was jammed. On the dance floor set up in front of the steel band, couples were barely able to move to the music.

I looked toward the side gate, thinking about my escape.

Even though the party had been confined to the house and surrounding gardens, there was no way to contain the noise and excitement. Earlier a crowd of onlookers had gathered outside the garden walls, hoping to catch a glimpse of the celebrities as they arrived. We had had to hire guards expressly for the purpose of keeping an eye on the passersby and keeping out the uninvited guests. It was late now and I was glad to see that the curious had dispersed and that the guards had come in to sit over coffee in the kitchen in case they were needed later on. The street at the side of the house was almost deserted.

For me, it was the moment of opportunity. There would be no one to register surprise at seeing the hostess of this reception in street clothes. Even the housekeeper was busy taking care of the coat check. If she did catch a glimpse of someone coming down the stairs carrying an overcoat, I hoped she would simply assume that it was one of the maids going home.

I headed for the house, intending to go straight to my room, but as I pressed through the people mingling around the dance floor, I noticed my husband dancing closely with his current favorite, Sylvia Gaylord.

He caught my eye and signaled that he wanted to talk to me. With a brief shake of my head, I refused and continued to make my way past. But he wasn't about to leave it at that. "Vivian," he called out, pushing his way through the crowd. "Stop."

"What do you want?" I asked. "I really can't think of anything that could be as important as dancing with Sylvia." My mood wasn't improved any by the smarting of my toes. I tried to soothe the ache by shifting my weight impatiently from one foot to another.

"Cut the crap, Vivian. I don't want it and I don't need it.

I'm just delivering a message, okay? I've been told there's someone wanting to talk to you. Something to do with your brother, of all things."

"My brother? But my brother's in Africa! What on earth could—"

"That's your problem," he snapped. "I just wish that you would take care of it. I'm damn tired of being interrupted."

"Oh, so sorry to disturb you, master," I said scornfully. "I suppose that my brother might be dying or something, but you're not to be disturbed."

"That's right," he said, almost spitting, and he was gone, back into the crowd and into Sylvia's arms.

I was shaken. We had never been so openly hateful. At last, I thought, I was going to be free.

"Will you have a glass of champagne with me?" asked a voice close beside me. It was a young lawyer, a friend of my husband's.

"Thank you," I replied with a smile. "Not just now. I have to run upstairs and see that everything is all right. Later, perhaps."

Outwardly, I was managing to appear quite calm. Inside, I was feeling more and more turmoil.

Once inside the house I slipped toward the stairs. Suddenly I was confronted by one of the waiters who had been hired for the night.

"Someone is asking for you, madam."

I was so caught up in the battle with Martin and my struggle to get out of the house as planned that I had forgotten completely about Martin's strange message.

"Who?" I asked. The young man was a stranger to me. I assumed he was part of the temporary staff taken on just for the party. He was holding a small tray in one hand.

"Who is it?" I asked again.

He shook his head and took a step back, appearing to be quite anxious to get back to his job. "I don't know, madam," he replied. "I was crossing the courtyard on my way into the house to get some ice and a woman at the front gate called to me. She asked me to tell you that she wanted to speak to you."

"As you sure she means me?"

"She distinctly said, 'Mrs. Fawkes.' She also said that it was quite urgent. Something to do with your brother, she said. Otherwise I wouldn't have bothered you. . . ."

"My brother? Are you sure she said my brother?"

"She said, 'Tell Mrs. Fawkes that I must speak to her about her brother, Simon.'"

"How curious," I said. I was, in fact, quite taken aback. Very few people knew that I had a brother, much less that his name was Simon. After a struggle through which he'd overcome the severe paralysis caused by an accident in his youth, Simon had dedicated himself to becoming a missionary doctor. He'd been working in Africa for several years, and we occasionally exchanged letters, but that was the extent of it. Was he trying to contact me? If so, why in this strange manner? And why now?

"What do you want me to do?" the waiter asked. "Should I tell—"

I interrupted him impatiently. "Tell the woman I'll see her."

And still the waiter hesitated.

"Well?" I urged.

"The woman doesn't want to come in because she's not dressed," he said quickly.

"This is ridiculous!" I exclaimed, making no effort to keep the annoyance out of my tone. "She doesn't have to be in an evening gown just to come and speak to me. Look, tell her I'll meet her at the side entrance."

"But she doesn't want to come in, even into the garden," he insisted. "It seems she has an urgent message and has to deliver it to you personally. She said it would only take a second."

"How do you know she won't come to the side entrance? You haven't even asked her yet."

"Er, yes, but I did. I knew you wouldn't want to talk to her out at the gate."

In spite of myself, I was intrigued. I didn't quite know what to do. "I'd better go and find out what this is all about," I said finally.

The waiter turned on his heel and disappeared into the crowd. I grabbed a wrap and threw it around my shoulders. As I hurried outside, I suddenly realized that my shoes were still hurting me.

The front of the house was lit by a series of spotlights cleverly hidden in the trees. I looked around me and couldn't help but be impressed by the total effect. The decorators certainly had done an excellent job. The front courtyard was deserted, although strewn with the cups and paraphernalia that are evidence of an enjoyable party. The evening chill and late hour had drawn the more adventuresome to the rear of the house where the thronging crowd warmed themselves in rhythm to the intoxicating beat of the steel band. Over the cheerful party sounds of people talking and carrying on I thought I could hear Martin's distinctive laugh. The sounds of gaiety only made the loneliness of the front courtyard more noticeable.

Where is that woman? I thought, walking over the brick walkway to the ornate cast-iron gate.

"Hello? Is anybody there?" I called out softly.

No sooner had I spoken than I felt someone rush toward me. Before I had time to realize what was happening, two figures jumped at me out of the dark shadows of the bushes near the gate. In the next instant, I was held fast in the grasp of strong hands. I felt sick with panic. I struggled against the cold hands that gripped me harder and harder. I felt helpless. I opened my mouth to scream and a handkerchief was quickly stuffed in it. I couldn't make a sound. I began to feel dizzy. I saw the whites of a man's eyes standing out against dark hair, dark skin...and white ...white.... Then everything started swirling into a black pool, while the words *Why? Why? Why?* pounded in my ears.

Chapter 3

I had the impression that I was falling...falling.... It was not a pleasant feeling. I seemed to be in a dark, bottomless well...along the sides were some kind of branches or vines. I could feel them scratching me as I fell. My body felt like a ton of lead. When would it all stop? I was choking with terror....

Finally, I received a sudden jolt. It seemed that I had reached the bottom. Immediately, I was overwhelmed by a nauseating odor and I couldn't move. I was absolutely paralyzed. I made a desperate effort to lift my arm. It was useless. I remained quite motionless, my head whirling.

My instinct toward self-preservation, however, was still very much alive. I knew I had to get out of there somehow—and fast.

I opened my eyes only slightly and then quickly closed them again. What I had seen didn't make any sense at all. Was I having some kind of a nightmare? As I lay there, unable to move, I felt more like a spectator than a participant in this strange twilight world.

With a sigh, I opened my eyes again. It had to be a dream. The room I was in was totally foreign. The windows had white curtains and there were lamps on the walls. The table was covered with an embroidered cloth, and what appeared to be an old-fashioned porch swing stood off to one side. The cut flowers in a crystal vase blazed in a glory of such extraordinary color that I could only assume I was seeing them in a dream. Through the open window, I caught sight of a profusion of greenery and flowers of remarkable colors. Deep reds, bright yellows, rich mauves...colors that seemed more dreamlike than real.

I rubbed my eyes and realized that my hands were moist. I was perspiring. The dream, it seemed, was ongoing. My surroundings had remained the same, with all their charm as well as their anomalies. The things around me seemed quite real. I told myself it was time to wake up.

Finally, I managed to lift myself on one elbow. I felt dizzy and sore all over and my stomach was in a knot. I realized that I was lying on a four-poster bed, complete with flowing canopy. I reached out and touched the material of the canopy. It was real. I was real. And I was awake.

With great effort I finally managed to sit up, hoping my head would clear. I felt very uneasy. No longer could I pretend that it was all a dream. What was it, then? Where was I?

I tried to reason with myself. I had to think back, try to remember everything that had happened. I had just awakened from a deep sleep—that much was obvious. Beyond that, my mind seemed to be a blank. I felt very confused. I couldn't remember anything that might relate to what was happening to me. I wondered if I might be suffering from amnesia. And yet, fragmented memories flashed across my mind; flashes of images, bits of conversations, figures, forms, places came and went, each staying for only the briefest of moments. It was all mixed together, making no sense at all, and then it was gone. Madness, I thought to myself, must surely begin with just this kind of incoherence.

And then a name came to mind. It worked like a key, opening a secret door. Things started to take shape. First, there was a figure...and then a face. I remembered lipstick, vivid red, on a laughing mouth. Sylvia! And I felt pain in my heart. Sylvia Gaylord, my husband's latest fling....

But hadn't I decided to put all of that behind me? Hadn't I planned to leave?

What had happened to all my careful planning? Hadn't my decision to run away been made only after many hours of anguish? Then why hadn't I carried out my plans? Why hadn't I simply left?

Gingerly, I lowered my feet to the floor and tried to stand up. My head felt very light and my mind seemed to be in a fog. What had happened to me? How had I got here?

I fell back on the bed with a sigh. Suddenly I realized that I was not alone in the room. I looked up to see a woman standing beside my bed. Confused and bewildered, mute and wide-eyed, I stared at her. Somehow I sensed that everything was tied together. Was this strange dream I was experiencing at the moment part of what had happened at the reception? The beautiful dark-skinned face I was looking at, the unusual costume the woman standing next to me was wearing, the angular figure. . . . It all took me back to the tropical setting that had been the subject of so many compliments at the reception.

There was no doubt about the authenticity of the woman. Everything about her was definitely West Indian. And very real. Just as real as she had been at the party, serving punch to our guests, her face smiling under her bandanna, the flower in her hair exactly like the one she was wearing now. But how did she get there? How did she get here? How did I get here?

I shivered. There was no logic, no reason, to anything that had happened. Wasn't I in New York? If I wasn't, where was I? I shook my head, hoping to make the apparition disappear. I closed my eyes.

When I opened them again, the woman was still there. She made a gesture, as though to point to herself, and spoke. "I'm Lucille," she said in a soft, clear voice.

Was I losing my mind? I could do nothing but stare at her.

"Are you awake?" she asked. Her dark eyes seemed to look right through me. "Do you need anything? Would you like a drink? Something to eat, perhaps? A little fruit . . . ?"

I shook my head once more. It was all quite impossible. No dream could ever be as real as this. "Where am I?" I asked, my voice shaky.

The woman seemed surprised by the question and hesitated a moment before speaking. "You mean here?" she asked, indicating the room with a sweeping gesture of her hand.

I managed to swing my legs over the side of the bed so that I could sit up and face the stranger. "Of course, here! How did I get here?"

My mind was still very confused. I was thoroughly

puzzled and disoriented, and I could feel my irritation increasing by the minute. I was wearing a simple cotton nightgown I had never seen before...and nothing else. Who had undressed me? Where were my clothes? Whose nightgown was this? Where was I? These questions and others ran through my whirling and groggy mind in a jumble.

The woman looked at me with curiosity and puzzlement. I didn't know her—or did I? Who was she? Why wouldn't she answer my questions?

"Why am I here?" I asked, trying another approach, my voice still shaky and sounding more like some stranger's. What was wrong with me?

The woman lifted her shoulders in a gesture that indicated she didn't understand the question. At that moment, I suddenly recalled the darkness of the garden near the gate, the hands clutching me....

My God, I thought to myself. *I've been kidnapped!*

The woman stood motionless before me, smiling. Who was she? She seemed kind and as if she wanted to be helpful. I couldn't believe that she might be one of "them"—yet why else would she be in this room with me? Might she harm me?

"Where am I?" I demanded again, growing desperate to get some answer from her, some piece of reality that I could hang on to. "Please, I want to know why I've been kidnapped! Tell me. Tell me something!" Crying, I clenched my fists and held them against my head in frustration.

My emotional outburst had an unexpected effect on the young woman. She stared at me as though I were some kind of devil and then suddenly turned and made a dash for the door.

"Wait!" I cried.

But she was gone. My only reply was the click of the latch as the door closed behind her. I tried to get up to follow her, but I didn't have the strength. My head began to spin and I fell back on the bed, unable even to put two thoughts together.

I stayed there without moving, trying to catch my breath. Gradually I calmed down and my thoughts became clear once more. I closed my eyes so as not to be distracted by my strange surroundings and tried to think back to the events that had brought me to this mysterious place. Certain details came to me as clear as daylight. The house, the people, the lights, the noise...my husband dancing with Sylvia Gaylord, holding her close in his arms. The waiter in the hallway telling me that someone was asking for me at the front gate. My rush to reach that dark area of the garden and then...the sudden attack, the gag in my mouth, the choking sensation. And most of all the terror, the feeling of complete helplessness. I remembered it all.

Of course, I had been kidnapped. Before I had been able to carry out my plan to run away, I had been snatched from my home and carried to a strange place. By whom? For what purpose?

I thought of Martin. Had he set this thing up, having somehow become aware of my intention to leave? Or was he trying to get rid of me, not knowing that I was leaving in any case? What other reasons could he have? I was baffled.... Worse, I was becoming frightened. What could I expect to happen next?

Things like this happened to other people. Not to me. But the reality was there. I was indeed in a strange room, and in a strange tropical land by the look of it. It certainly was not New York City, that I was sure of. The gentle feel of the breeze coming through the window, the intoxicating fragrance of flowers, the bright colors, were very definitely not part of the early October landscape on Long Island.

A wisp of a memory passed by and I struggled to hold on to it. What was it that the air and fragrance of this place reminded me of? Something quite pleasant...something free.... Yes, I had it—it was that tropical holiday on which Martin had sent me when he felt the need to be discreet about his affairs. He managed his rendezvous at that time by sending me out of the country for several weeks, under the guise of being the generous, loving husband that he never was.

I had quite unexpectedly fallen in love with the tropics. That was a long time ago, over six years, and the caressing, soothing breezes were bringing back to me the pleasure I had found on that first and last holiday. I struggled to remember where it was that Martin had sent me, and what, exactly, the place had been like. I remembered that it had been private and secluded—naturally, Martin wanted to have his fun knowing full well that I wouldn't have the chance to be tempted by male company. Was I in the tropics? So far everything I had seen and experienced told me that I was.

A sudden fragment of a memory jolted me so that I sat bolt upright, in spite of my grogginess. I remembered the way Martin had come away from the dance floor, leaving Sylvia Gaylord behind, insistent on telling me that I had to get the message at the gate. Why had he gone out of his way? Surely he must have been in on the scheme or he wouldn't have bothered. But why? In so many ways, the whole thing seemed absurd.

Could Martin actually be behind this cruel scheme? We didn't love each other; in fact, we probably hated each other by now. But there wasn't enough emotion between us to justify this kind of cruelty. Would he actually be putting me through this nightmare? And why?

I knew that he was quite capable of being ruthless in his business dealings when he was sure there was no way that anyone would find out about it. On more than one occasion he had condemned a family to poverty by blacklisting them in New York. I even knew of one case in which he subtly got what he wanted from a woman by threatening to expose her past history as a prostitute to her upstanding husband.

Martin wasn't, by any means, the generous and people-loving man he wanted society to see him as. He was quite capable of being terribly cruel, and even enjoying it. But I never thought that his cruel streak would be turned against me.

I wondered how long I'd been asleep. I looked at my wrist and was somewhat surprised to see that my watch was still there. According to the dial, it was ten o'clock on Sunday, October 6th.

The party had been on Saturday, on October 5th. As nearly as I could calculate, I was attacked shortly after midnight. I had been unconscious almost ten hours, and could remember nothing of that time. What had happened? How far from New York had they carried my unconscious body?

I was overcome by a wave of bitterness at the thought that Martin probably was behind all this. What was he hoping to gain? What were his intentions? More and more, I was becoming convinced that he was the one responsible for this cruel travesty. With the help, of course, of a few discreet friends. My husband knew so many people, some of whom were as cold-blooded as he was, that I was quite sure he was convinced he could do anything and get away with it. *But this time*, I thought to myself, *he's gone too far.*

I managed to drag myself out of bed, determined to find out what was going on. With faltering steps, I walked toward the open window, recalling something that my husband had said: "Why aren't you wearing your emeralds?" Had he known that I had sold my jewels to raise the money required for my escape? If he had found out, he must have been furious. Perhaps he had set up this apparent kidnapping to teach me a lesson. But I still didn't know what he expected to gain by it.

I reached the open window and felt the balmy breeze against my face. Suddenly my anger dissipated. With great surprise and not a little admiration, I looked out upon glorious scenery that was quite unlike anything I had ever seen before. There seemed to be multicolored flowers everywhere. It was decidedly a tropical setting, with exotic plants and vegetation, but more beautiful than anything I had ever experienced.

In the distance I could make out the tiny figures of people working the land. It seemed to be some sort of plantation. Here and there amid the vibrant greenery was a small house with a red roof. Beyond the plantation I could make out what appeared to be a green sea.

"How beautiful!" I murmured aloud.

"Do you really think so?"

The voice from behind me made me jump in surprise. Quickly, I turned around to face a strange woman. She was blond, and although she was casually dressed in jeans and a subtly fashionable T-shirt, she was obviously very careful about her appearance. As a former fashion model, I was aware of the amount of time and skill it took to achieve a certain polished look—and this woman, who seemed to be about my age, had it. Her hair was attractively styled and her makeup skillfully applied to bring out her natural beauty, which was considerable, without the makeup itself being noticeable at all. Strands of fine gold circled her neck, and through the profusion of fair hair that fell to her shoulders I could see the glint of tiny gold earrings. Her naturally fair skin had taken on a golden color in the tropical climate.

On first impression, this stranger was someone I liked and wanted to befriend. It was, therefore, with some effort that I reminded myself of my circumstances, that she was most likely one of "them" and that I should, above all else, respond with caution.

"I see that you finally woke up," she said in an amused tone.

"Who are you?" I asked bluntly.

"I live here," she replied. "I'm the household manager."

I looked at her, confused. It hadn't been much of an answer. It didn't tell me anything about what was really going on.

"Lucille told me that you were awake," she continued. "I came as quickly as I could. I'm sure you must be very hungry. You'll find that we have everything you may need here." She indicated a small table on which there was a large tray of fruit and a tall decanter. "Please sit down and help yourself," she urged.

Dumbfounded, I allowed myself to be led to the table. I realized suddenly that I was very thirsty. I picked up a glass and held it as the young woman poured the liquid from the decanter. It was cool and cloudy.

"This is one of our native drinks," she explained. "It's a mixture of fruit juices and coconut milk."

"Thank you," I replied uncertainly.

"Please...do sit down," she repeated, pulling out the chair on the opposite side of the table for herself. I sat down across from her and she put a plate in front of me. With extraordinary grace, she delicately cut a slice of pineapple.

"You must be starving. How did you feel when you woke up?" she inquired.

I sat looking at her, wondering if she was making fun of me. She seemed so natural, so candid, yet I couldn't quite believe that her apparent innocence could be genuine.

"I really would like to know what I'm doing here." I was making every effort to keep my tone light, yet it still revealed a note of exasperation. Surely she could understand that I was finding this whole situation quite incomprehensible.

"For the time being, all you have to worry about is getting your strength back," she replied, apparently concentrating on peeling the banana she held in her hands.

I waved my hand in a gesture of impatience. "That's not true. I'm much more concerned about getting some kind of explanation."

It seemed, however, that I was alone in my concern. Her expression remained quite pleasant, completely unworried. "Listen," she said. "Let's get one thing straight. I'm not going to provide any explanations—that isn't why I'm here. It's my job to look after you and make sure you have everything you want."

I was becoming more and more angry. "This is ridiculous! I've been kidnapped, drugged, taken by force from one place to another. I don't know where I am or why I'm here. Yet you refuse to give me any explanation."

She arched her eyebrows, staring at me. "That's not

true. You were not kidnapped. That much I know for sure."

"But you know I was!" I snapped.

"You're just imagining things. You were not kidnapped," she replied slowly, as if to a child. Her tone was quite calm, her expression unchanged.

"Well, let me tell you, this whole thing is getting more than a little annoying. I don't know where I am or how I got here. I'm beginning to wonder if I even know who I am!"

She looked me straight in the eye. "Why would anyone want to kidnap you?"

"Oh, come now," I retorted, my voice rising in spite of my intentions to remain calm. "You know perfectly well that I was kidnapped! I'm sure you must know my husband and are quite aware of the extent to which he is capable of going. I'm convinced that he's at the bottom of this little maneuver. Well, this time he's gone too far! No matter what he might think, he's simply not above the law. I may be his wife, but we're not living in the Middle Ages. He's going to have to answer for this, believe me, and anyone else who might be involved will be brought to justice, as well."

My extreme agitation and defiant attitude left little doubt that I truly meant every word I was saying. I sat glaring at the young woman and was astonished to see a glint of amusement appear in her eyes. Then the corners of her mouth lifted in a faint smile. The whole thing, it seemed, was quite amusing to her. Well, it wasn't to me. I became even more furious.

"Please calm down. I assure you that there's no truth in what you say. You have certainly not been kidnapped. You are here by choice. So relax," she replied calmly.

"I don't believe you," I exclaimed. "For one thing, you must know who asked you to look after me. And you must know who this house belongs to."

She threw up her hands in a gesture of helplessness. "All I can tell you is what I know," she said.

"Then tell me!" I demanded.

"All I know is that you are a guest in this house and you arrived last night. You are the wife of a friend of the owner, and you are to receive special medical attention and lots of rest. I was asked to look after you when you woke up. I'm at your disposal, you see. It's up to me to see that you have everything you might need. This morning I had Lucille standing by at your bedside. Her orders were to advise me the minute you woke up."

"But what do you mean—special medical attention? There isn't anything wrong with me!"

"I'm afraid that you'll have to talk to the doctor about that. I'm not qualified to discuss it with you."

"But surely you must know something. Please, tell me. I must know!"

"Again, I'm sorry to have to agitate you, but I'm under orders not to discuss this matter with you in any way."

She was firm in her stand. I realized that I would gain no information if I tried to pursue the subject further. And she hadn't told me anything. I was almost beside myself. "How did I get here?" I asked abruptly.

"By plane, of course."

"By plane?"

"It's the only way to get here," she replied. "No, I shouldn't say that. You could have come by ship. But there hasn't been a ship in port for several days. In any event, I do know that a plane from the United States landed here last night."

I jumped up from my chair. "So this isn't the United States!"

"Of course it isn't," she laughed. "This is an island, part of the archipelago."

"Part of the what?"

"You're on an island in the Caribbean, can't you tell?" Her hand indicated the lush growth just outside the open window. "Mind you, ours is a very small island. So small, in fact, that it doesn't even appear on some maps. But on a clear day we can see all the other islands around us in the Caribbean Sea—provided we want to take the trouble to go to the mountains to look around. Actually, we're very well located here."

I was ready to burst. The vegetation, the trees, the exotic flowers.... I had realized before that I was in some tropical country, but the reality, the blunt truth, still came as a shock to me. I couldn't believe my ears. "I'm in the middle of the Caribbean?" I repeated stupidly.

"Just about. You're on St. Victor Island, which belongs to James de Vergoff."

"I've never heard of him." Then I stopped to think for a second. It had to be some friend of Martin's. She had said I was "the wife of a friend of the owner," hadn't she? This was certainly a possibility. However, I knew very few of Martin's friends.

I was becoming frustrated almost to the point of insanity. Angrier than ever, I was almost ready to jump across the table at the young woman, but I realized that I had to play it cool. After all, appearances and words to the contrary, the innocent-looking woman was probably one of my kidnappers. For a moment I stopped and glared at her. "Where is...what's his name? James de...? When can I see him?"

She burst into laughter. "It isn't all that easy to see him," she said. "He's a very busy, very powerful man. In any case, he isn't here at the moment."

"Then where is he?"

"Out there somewhere, on the plantation. As soon as he gets back, I'll tell him that you want to see him."

"Yes, I do want to see him. And since you claim that I have not been kidnapped, you won't have any objections if I talk to whatever authorities there might be on this island. There must be some kind of police force, some court system around here," I said, trying to appear matter-of-fact and calm about things.

"Of course I wouldn't object, if your doctor approved. However, the only authority on this island is the boss. He's the mayor, the fire chief, the police officer—you name it. He owns the island, you see, and anyone who lives here has to go to him whenever there happens to be a complaint."

I couldn't believe it. My insides were churning as my sense of rebellion increased. "Whoever this man is, he must have to account for his actions to some kind of authority!"

"That's not what I said. There is an authority. This island is under the jurisdiction of the colonial office, which is set up on one of the other islands. Nevertheless, to all intents and purposes, deVergoff is the authority here."

"What about this doctor business? I suppose that I *will* see a doctor?" I was trying to sound very sure of myself, but I couldn't quite control the trembling in my voice. Somehow this mysterious medical situation frightened me more than anything else. But I had to see someone, gather more information, even if only the slightest bits of fact. Perhaps seeing the so-called doctor would help fit together some of the pieces of this puzzle.

"I'll inquire about that for you," she said, getting to her feet. I could only assume that she was thinking she had done enough talking.

"I'll let you take your bath and get dressed now," she said quietly. She moved her head slightly to indicate a large chest of drawers. "You'll find clothing suitable for the tropics in the dresser. I put some things there while you were sleeping this morning. The evening gown you were wearing when you arrived is in the closet. It's very elegant, but not too appropriate in this climate."

I should have thanked her for her efforts, but I was unable to speak.

"By the way," she added, "I'm Christine. Forgive me for not introducing myself earlier. As I mentioned before, I'm the household manager. My husband oversees the estate. Please understand that everything here is at your disposal. If you need anything, ring this bell and Lucille will look after it. You are free to come and go as you please. In spite of what you believe, you are not a prisoner here."

I was dumbfounded. She spoke with such conviction and warm sincerity that I found it hard not to believe what she said was true.

She turned gracefully and headed for the door. Then she stopped and turned back to face me, smiling. "And remember, you are here for a rest, so be sure to relax and enjoy yourself. Take a bath. It will refresh you. Sleep, read, rest...whatever you please. We are your friends, believe me."

Then she left, and I was alone again with my confusion and unanswered questions.

Chapter 4

The sound of my visitor's footsteps on the tiles lingered outside the door of my room. Suddenly I felt quite alone. What had just happened had left me perplexed and very uneasy. It was all quite incredible and yet apparently it was very real.

There were too many questions and too few answers. I was in complete darkness and began to feel a paralyzing terror. But, having always been a fighter, I struggled against the fear that threatened to overcome me and managed to control it. Christine had suggested a bath. Well, I certainly could use one. Perhaps it would help to straighten out my head. At any rate, it would do me a lot of good.

I started to explore my room. It was large, bright and spacious. The gentle breeze coming through the open windows played gracefully with the tasteful floral drapes that matched the fabric on the canopy of the bed. It was both elegant and comfortable, a combination hard to achieve. I waltzed around the room, unexpectedly uplifted from the realities of my situation by the grace and beauty of my prison. I ran my finger over the perfectly waxed surfaces of the antique desk, chest of drawers and hope chest.

One louvered set of wooden doors led me into a bathroom that was large and luxurious in the manner that only a century-old bathroom could be. The fixtures and decor, however, were sparkling new and of an unusual design; the room was modern to the point of being quite sumptuous. There was a sunken bathtub, very large and shaped in an oval. Assorted oils, perfumes and exotic herbs were lined up along a built-in shelf close to the bath, and a bright floral silk robe and slender sandals were placed nearby. At the edge of the bath, on an enamel tray, was a tasty-looking arrangement of fruits, nuts and cheeses, as well as a slender glass of what looked to be wine or juice.

I was overwhelmed. The thought and care that I was being given was beyond imagining. Clearly, this was a spot in which to relax and enjoy oneself . . . but why? Why was I being treated both so violently and so tenderly at the same time? The contradiction between what I was experiencing and what I knew to be the reality of the situation—that I was a victim of a cruel and frightening kidnapping—tormented me. Was I mad? What was going on?

Shaking my head to clear my thoughts, I continued my exploration. Everything I saw only reinforced my astonishment over the luxury and beauty of my surroundings. All the bathroom fixtures were of a matching robin's egg blue porcelain. An antique circular vanity with a delicate floral design etched into the lacquered finish stood in front of a gilt-edged oval mirror. Glistening plants cascaded in front of the open window that looked out on a mountain. To the right were louvered doors that opened onto shelves of lush, matching floral towels and linens.

But it was when I opened the door next to the built-in shower that I got my biggest surprise—and a pleasant one to be sure. It was a large, cedar-lined sauna, steaming and ready for my use. These were indeed luxurious quarters for a prisoner!

I decided that a relaxing sauna and bath would do me a great deal of good. In the oval mirror I could see the tension reflected in my pale face. My usually shiny black hair hung limp and lifeless. In spite of the fact that I had been unconscious for so long, dark circles surrounded my green eyes—the green eyes Martin had once found so pleasing...or so he had said. Well, if Martin had decided to play a game, at least he had chosen a jail that was anything but sordid. My surroundings seemed rather more like some kind of heaven than any kind of hell.

After a wonderful sauna, I stayed in the warm, perfumed water of my bath for a long time. When I finally did get out, I felt much better. My mind seemed clearer and I decided to attempt to put things together.

Why would Martin have sent me here? If he had really wanted to hurt me, he wouldn't have chosen a setting of such exotic charm. Should I be expecting him to join me here? Was he expecting to have a second honeymoon with me in this romantic place that might easily be considered to have been created expressly for lovers? I could consider this hypothesis only with repugnance. I didn't love Martin. Had I ever really loved him? We had been married for seven years. I had changed a great deal in those seven years. No longer was I the young woman Martin had married.

I met Martin Fawkes in a high-class New York restaurant. He was presiding over a panel of experts who had gathered to select a candidate to be the heroine of an illustrated romance that his newspaper was planning to publish. I was very young then, and without much experience in life. I had had to drop out of university only a few months before, and had just started my quickly blooming career as a high-fashion model. My agent had insisted that I compete in this contest—she had said it would be helpful for my career. And I certainly wasn't scornful of the money I might win.

In any case, the contest had intrigued me. More than anything, I looked upon it as a possible opportunity for new and exciting ventures. I might become famous—get into theater, television...even films.

Martin Fawkes, on the other hand, was a powerful, very wealthy man even then. He was a director of many companies, both local and international, and the publisher of a very successful newspaper. When I realized he was casting an eye my way with more than average interest, I had to admit that it made my head spin for a while. Although he was sixteen years older than I was, I found him very attractive. In fact, his maturity interested me all the more.

Since I was becoming one of the top fashion models in New York, my old friends, particularly the men, were shying away. They assumed that I had hordes of people around me at all times, all more interesting and exciting than they were. There were people around me, but none of them were friends and I didn't particularly find them interesting. In fact, I was spending a great deal of my private time alone, and I was beginning to feel quite lonely.

Martin's attention, then, was welcomed, not only because of the exciting type of life to which he introduced me, but because I wanted a friend. But I hadn't counted on being swept off my feet. As a student I had been accustomed to going to a movie dutch treat, and then going to a friend's to talk, or out for a beer. Courtship Martin-Fawkes-style was another matter altogether! Going to a first-class restaurant in a chauffeur-driven Jaguar was quite a bit different from using the subway to go to some local greasy spoon. And when we went to a special celebrity party on Long Island on one of his luxury yachts, I was, admittedly, charmed.

Nevertheless, I had spent most of my life in a small town, and my sense of values had remained intact. I refused to stand in awe of him and his world. I treated him just as I would anyone else. I wanted to get to know him, and I suppose he found this refreshing.

But mostly, I think, looking back on that time, he was attracted to the fact that I was becoming a highly coveted fashion model. Whenever we were together, he wanted to make sure we were seen.

I was surprised when he proposed. I hadn't been expecting it. I was flattered and warmed to think that he loved me—which I assumed he did. Why else would he ask me to marry him?

And I? What had my feelings been? Awe, I decided, together with blind infatuation, which I had mistaken for love. With the highest expectations I had married who I believed to be a man of great substance, only to discover later that I was the wife of a playboy. My husband eventually showed himself to be a master of deceit, behind whose every act of generosity lurked an ulterior motive. And after seven years of so-called marriage—our conjugal life together was so minimal that using the term *marriage* to describe it borders on exaggeration—I'd had ample opportunity to perceive that Martin was really quite incapable of any kind of true feeling.

I dried myself vigorously with a huge towel and, with an effort, pulled my thoughts back to the present. I had to find a way out of this trap.

From the huge closet I chose a dress of lightweight cotton with short sleeves. It was quite beautiful, as were the other clothes in the closet. The exclusive Paris designer labels on them didn't go unnoticed. It occurred to me that it had been very decent of Christine to take the trouble to select such attractive things for me to wear. If she hadn't, I'd have been left with nothing but the evening dress and wrap I had arrived in. The assortment and variety were quite pleasing, but what I found almost disturbing, certainly disquieting, was the fact that all of the clothes were in my size. Quickly, on an impulse, I opened the dresser drawers. There, as I had imagined, were all the underthings and other items that I needed for a complete wardrobe—and all in my size.

That was going too far! I felt trapped in an eerie magic fairyland, where everything was perfect but nothing made sense.

With trepidation I looked for shoes. There, at the bottom of the closet, under the large assortment of dresses, blouses and skirts, was a line of the finest-quality shoes to suit every occasion. At the end of the row, looking a bit worse for wear, was the pair of shoes I'd had the misfortune to wear the night of the party—the shoes that had pained me so. Cautiously, yet somehow knowing what I was going to find out, I slipped into one of the new pairs of shoes.

I couldn't help but laugh. Of course, they would fit me better than my own shoes did. I decided that a sense of humor was going to be necessary. And why not enjoy this experience? Relaxed after a sauna, freshly bathed and perfumed, I decided that, if nothing else, I was going to enjoy my kidnapping to the hilt. With pleasure I tried on several of the outfits, finally choosing one that especially suited me. It was a hot pink sun dress, pencil-thin, with buttons down the front and narrow straps over the shoulders. A slim belt emphasized my small waist. The color contrasted well with my green eyes and my now clean, shiny black hair that cascaded to my shoulders in natural curls.

Then I flopped down on the old-fashioned couch swing and, swinging gently in the breeze and gazing out at the view, I thought about my strange predicament.

I wondered if what Christine had said was true—that I was not a prisoner here, that I was entirely free to walk around the premises. There was only one way to find out, and as far as I could see, I had nothing to lose. I decided that the time had come to leave the security of my gem of a nest to explore.

I opened the door. I quickly found that my rooms were connected to a gallery that ran around the outside of the house. As soon as I stepped outside, I felt the incredible heat. I had not noticed that the interior of the house was air-conditioned, even though the windows were opened to let in the fresh air. The old place definitely had been converted to provide all the comforts of modern living.

A staircase from the gallery led to a swimming pool that seemed to be deserted for the moment. I could hear sounds coming from the house and saw men and women in native dress going back and forth. As they passed by, they nodded and murmured greetings with a smile. In spite of myself, my anger began to disappear.

With some caution, I continued to explore the area for

about half an hour. The lush gardens were quite marvelous and I had the sense of being completely alone. I was sure that if anyone was watching me, I'd have felt it.

Suddenly, a jeep came up the driveway and stopped in front of the house. Obeying an impulse to be careful, I quickly hid behind a clump of trees and watched. A tall, slender man, dressed in white, got out of the jeep. When he turned to shut the door, he was facing my direction.

It was the mysterious stranger I had seen dressed in a white dinner jacket at the reception! The same man, precisely, whom Sandra had been so eager to interview.

My heart leaped. Now I had proof that there was collusion between this man and my husband. He was at our house in New York at the time I had been kidnapped. Surely he must have been involved in Martin's plot and was there to finalize the details with him.

My mind was like a kaleidoscope as images twisted and turned. I could see the waiter telling me that someone was asking to see me at the gate. Another accomplice. The whole thing was carefully choreographed. My anger resurfaced with renewed vigor, and I had to restrain myself from calling out, "Wait!"

The tall stranger rushed across the gallery and disappeared inside the house. Was this the James deVergoff Christine had mentioned, the owner of this island and my kidnapper? I decided to follow close behind, to see if I could learn something new. He was walking quickly and appeared too preoccupied to notice me. I continued to follow him quietly as he opened doors and hurried from room to room through the vast house. Finally he reached a room and closed the door behind him.

I wasn't sure what to do. I was down the hall, hidden somewhat in the entrance to another room. Judging from the books and toys, it was a child's room. Undecided, I stopped for a moment. I was tempted to walk right in after the man, but something about the atmosphere intimidated me and I decided to be more careful. Also, it would be wiser for me to see what information I could gather before jumping right into the thick of things.

I looked around to see if there was anyone else in the hallway. I was alone. Downstairs the women were talking, and the noise of parakeets seemed to be coming from everywhere. In the heat of the day, the workers must have gone home. As far as the eye could see, the plantation was deserted.

Suddenly I heard a noise and I jumped back into the safety of the room. The door had opened and I could hear his footsteps coming my way. My heart was pounding. Although I had been told that I was allowed to walk around the premises, hiding behind doors and spying on people could not be regarded kindly. I held my breath as I watched him walk by. My attention was caught by his coal black hair, his bronze skin, his light blue eyes flashing with agitation. . . .

Another memory surfaced, making my knees weak and a moan surface in my throat quite against my wishes. As I covered my mouth with my hands to repress any sound I might make, I remembered a glimpse I had had of black hair and flashing eyes when I was attacked at the gate. It had been this man who had kidnapped me, whose hands had coldly grabbed me and whose face I saw just as my mind was reeling out of consciousness!

The memory of that attack made me shiver and tremble. I listened for the sound of his footsteps to fade into silence before I came out of my refuge. Timidly, I stepped into the hallway. He was nowhere in sight—no one was. The house sounded empty.

I wanted to go back to the safety of my room and rest, at least until I had got over the trembling. I was still feeling shaken at having seen and recognized my abductor. However, I knew I had to press on. Time was slipping by, and it was vital that I learn something about what was happening to me.

In spite of my beating heart, I knew what I had to do. I had to go into the room out of which he had just come.

Quickly I went to the door, opened it and slipped in, closing the door firmly behind me. The room was a study, elegantly and comfortably designed, with wood paneling and handsome, masculine furniture. Briefly, I thought with horror what it would be like to be caught by him in this room, but I forced myself to put such imaginings out of my mind.

I crossed over to the desk, clean and imposing with no telltale clutter for me to examine. The one item on the desk was a framed photograph of a handsome young woman holding a little boy of about three or four. It struck me as being quite different from the usual executive family portrait. It wasn't stiff or self-consciously posed. The woman radiated warmth and happiness, and the child had a sweet manner of expression that was both impish and absolutely lovable at the same time. I wondered if the woman and child lived on the island, hoping, in fact, that they did. How could one feel threatened or frightened in such a warm family atmosphere?

But one thought of that man's ice blue eyes brought me back to reality. Quickly, without rearranging anything, I looked through the drawers of the desk. Nothing. Only the usual office supplies, carefully arranged. I noticed a stack of business cards: James deVergoff, President, The Mills. So it was *his* study. But he couldn't use his desk much, I thought. The contents were so orderly it seemed that they hadn't been moved recently.

Were there no files in this study? I looked around the room. There were none in sight, but something caught my attention. It was a large shelving unit, unusually wide. I realized that it must disguise something other than books. I examined the front of it for a break in the wood, and it didn't take long to notice two small wood knobs at the center. Without any effort I swung the shelves open, revealing a row of filing cabinets.

I set to work, opening first one drawer and then another, scanning the file tags for some item that might be of interest to me. Several I opened, but they were standard business forms and contracts, having to do with the sale of produce and goods to clients on the other islands and in the United States. I could see nothing suspicious about them.

It was at the third drawer that my heart started to quicken at the possibility of finding some information. This was the Miscellany drawer, devoted to all and sundry that could not be readily filed. Right in the front, without any tag to proclaim it, but bulging with items, was a file containing all manner of information on Martin.

At last I had found the information I was looking for! I ruffled through the file. It was full of news clippings about Martin and a rather upsetting investigator's report describing the many romances Martin had had, as well as his usual daily business. This man must have been trailing Martin for months! I forced myself to skim the report, realizing that my life depended upon unraveling the pieces to this puzzle. I could not allow my personal feelings to interfere with my need for information. At the back of the file was an old news clipping that had nothing to do with Martin at all. Something about a car accident. I could only assume it had been misfiled.

I was pulled abruptly from my investigation by the sound of footsteps in the hallway. In a panic, I closed the file and the outside shelves and stood trembling at the side of the door. I was faint with relief as I heard the footsteps go past the room and down the hall, fading at last into silence. It was time for me to get out of the study before I got caught. I had learned enough . . . for the time being.

Chapter 5

With a stealthiness I didn't think was in me, I slipped out the door of James deVergoff's study, into the hall and up the stairs. It was with a tremendous sense of relief that I finally closed behind me the door to my room, welcoming its solitude with an almost animal pleasure.

During my absence refreshments had been brought in, another dish of fruit and some pastries. I wasn't at all hungry. But when I looked at my watch I realized I had been gone for more than an hour.

I was exhausted, and so confused I couldn't think. I tried to find some kind of perspective by going over in my mind everything that had happened. I had indeed found a link between James deVergoff and my husband. The existence of the file in deVergoff's study proved that there was some connection. However, certain questions were raised that were bothering me more than ever.

What was the nature of the relationship between Martin and James deVergoff? That was still a mystery. If they were friends, what purpose would be served in kidnapping me? Were they business associates? Was this some elaborate financial scheme? I had heard of a case in which a wealthy businessman had a member of his own family kidnapped so that he'd be able to claim an enormous loss on income taxes, thus saving himself from financial ruin. Was Martin in a financial bind? Had he rigged this sick scheme to save face financially? I knew that Martin would go to any lengths to maintain his social status—no doubt, the company he kept would not have patience with any but the high-rolling crowd. But would he go so far as to kidnap his own wife?

If this were the case, if James de Vergoff was a business associate who was cooperating with Martin in order to make money, why would he keep a file on Martin? Why had de Vergoff ordered— if, indeed, he had been the one to order it—the detective report? If James and Martin were friends, which was the theory I had been going on, why would James have Martin followed so closely for so many months? And how was I involved? Was he perhaps trying to blackmail Martin with the information he had turned up in the detective report? Was I part of a blackmail scheme?

One question led to another, and my head ached with the weight of unsolvable problems. My heart sank with yet another thought, perhaps the most frightening of them all: what if Martin were not involved in the kidnapping scheme? The thought chilled me to the bone, in spite of the warmth of the afternoon air. However odious it seemed to have one's own husband be the instigator of a kidnapping, at least I was dealing with an enemy I knew. The thought that I might be the victim of a straightforward, everyday kidnapping, if there was such a thing, was terrifying. If that were the case, then I was probably being held for ransom. Would my kidnappers threaten to kill me? Would Martin pay to free me, knowing that I had left him?

If Martin could be expected to feel anything at all, it would only be resentment. When the reception was over, he likely stormed upstairs, furious with me for not having been at his side to say good-night to our guests. And then he would have found the note I had pinned to his pillow. I thought of what I had written.

Martin, by the time you read this I'll be gone. After a lot of serious thought, I'm leaving you. I can't accept the life you've made for me any longer. I have to get out of this house, where I am nothing more than a decoration. My mind and my heart simply refuse to go on with the charade.

I am keeping the jewels you have given me. What I realize from selling them will be enough to get me started in a new, more normal life. I want nothing else.

Make no mistake about my own reasons for leaving. For what it's worth, there is no other man in my life. I'm going, quite simply, because I've had enough. I want only to find myself and once again feel some degree of self-respect.

When my life has become a little more organized, I'll retain a lawyer to make whatever arrangements are necessary to settle the situation between us. In the meantime, don't try to reach me. I have made very sure that no one will be able to find me until I choose to be found. From here on in, I'll be making all my own decisions.

I had weighed every word carefully before putting it

down and was quite sure the note must have angered Martin. Indeed, he would have been somewhat mortified, as well. How could the insignificant Vivian permit herself the luxury of scorning his generosity? He was rich and attractive, powerful and feared, a man any woman would have been proud to marry. And now Martin, the irresistible, was being cast aside . . . and by his own wife. He wouldn't be able to accept it.

I knew he would be hating me. But would his hate be so great that he'd leave me in danger of my life in the hands of kidnappers?

The very fact that I had left Martin and told him why was unknown to James deVergoff. It could prove to be the destruction of all my kidnapper's carefully laid plans. If my thinking was correct, the plantation owner was expecting an immediate reaction from Martin, imagining that my husband would be furious at the discovery that his beloved had disappeared. Such, however, would not be the case. Disgusted by my behavior, Martin probably wouldn't lift a finger.

The realization of how little my life meant to Martin shook me. Could it be true? Wouldn't he even come to my rescue if I were endangered? Having an unhappy marriage was one thing, but risking someone's life was quite another.

What should I do? I was torn with a sense of confused urgency. Should I tell my kidnapper that he had made a terrible mistake in taking me as his hostage? Should I explain to him that Martin would not make the slightest effort to get his wife back? But then, what would he do with me? Kill me? Surely he wouldn't let me go only to tell the world and convict him?

My head was throbbing with all the questions, the pieces

of the puzzle that would not come together. Was there nothing that made any sense in this place?

I was led to the window by the sound of singing. The clarity of the air and the brightness of the sun gave the landscape a lucid, sparkling color that shimmered with vibrancy. In the distance I could see men, women and children walking down the road, singing in harmony, their arms clasped affectionately.

I thought about James deVergoff. If he was my jailer, at least he was a generous one. He had provided me with an enchanting island for a prison. Without a doubt, it was the most beautiful place I could ever have imagined. There was peaceful quiet, space, harmony and natural beauty so luxurious as to be almost beyond belief. In all of my planning to leave home, I had never dreamed of escaping to such a marvelous place.

In a way, the whole thing was ironic. I had made a plan for freedom and now I was a prisoner. I had simply exchanged one kind of trap for another, except that from this one there seemed to be no escape.

Disgusted and weary, I stretched out on the bed. The day had been full, yet it wasn't nearly over. I still felt the tiring effects of the sedation, the drugs I had been given—whatever they were. My eyelids were heavy with exhaustion, and my mind and emotions ached for a respite from all that had happened.

I drifted into a state of blissful relaxation, oblivious to the concerns of my prison, aware only of the sounds of birds singing outside my window. In a very few minutes I was fast asleep.

Chapter 6

A knock on my door woke me. Groggily I called out, "Who is it?" But there was no answer except for another knock, and then another, more timid and gentle than the ones before it.

Curious, I went to the door and called out again, "Who is it?" Again there was no answer, but for the sounds of quietly shuffling feet and another timid knock, making almost a scratching sound.

Finally impatient, I opened the door to be surprised by a startled and frightened-looking Lucille, who seemed ready to bolt at the slightest hint of trouble from me.

"Is there anything madam wishes?" she asked nervously.

"No," I responded, still groggy. I looked at my watch: it was quite early in the afternoon. Although I had slept deeply, I had slept for only a very short time—no more than half an hour, if that. I shook my head, trying to clear it. "What about dinner?" I asked.

"It will be brought to your room in a few hours, if you wish," she reported dutifully.

"Yes, please. Is Christine in the house?" I wanted to find out more about the island and James deVergoff. I was also curious about what Christine had referred to as my "medical condition."

"No," Lucille replied shortly, turning on her heel and walking quickly away.

I thought it strange for a maid to be so jumpy, and I wondered what I had done to become so frightening to her. True, I had been emotional that morning when I awoke to find myself a victim of a kidnapping—but surely that was a perfectly understandable response. I hadn't attacked her, after all.

But I didn't let that thought bother me for long. The flood of questions was rushing through my mind again. I couldn't sit still and wait to see what would hapen; I had to find out more. It was possible that my life would be in danger if I didn't. Whether or not I was kidnapped by Martin or James deVergoff or both didn't change the fact that I had been kidnapped and was being held in this place—however beautiful it was—against my will. The time had come to escape. . . if I could.

I had a few free hours before I would be expected to be back for dinner, so I decided to go out and see what I could find. I splashed cold water on my face to freshen myself. I suspected that I was still under the influence of whatever drug it was that had put me to sleep for so long. I certainly didn't feel as energetic as I would have normally.

The oppressive heat outside didn't make me feel any more awake, but I pressed on, taking a path that circled around the pool and off into the thick jungle foliage.

The house was surrounded by a variety of colorful tropical flowers. There were fruit trees I had never seen before, laden with fruits I couldn't identify. The leaves on some of the trees were as colorful as the flowers. Exotic birds chirped and sang and flew in and out of the trees in all directions. The air in the forest was thick and humid, as in a greenhouse. Little light reached through the tall, protective trees, creating an underwater effect.

Coming from the man-made jungle of Manhattan, I was very much awed by the entirely natural world in the midst of which I suddenly found myself. Here, there could be no problems, no concern—only the beauty of nature and its music.

As I continued to walk I turned onto a new pathway, and quite suddenly all the charm of my surroundings was gone. In a wheelchair, being pushed by one of the local women, sat a small crippled child. The woman seemed surprised to see me and tried to avoid me. The child, watching me coming toward him, smiled.

I smiled back. "Hi!" I called out.

"Hello," he replied solemnly, his eyes wide with curiosity. "Stop, Mauricia!" he ordered.

Reluctantly the woman obeyed, mumbling a few words as she looked at me with obvious dislike.

"You're new here, aren't you?" asked the child.

He looked to be about six years old, and his cheerful, forward way of talking was charming coming from such a tiny boy. His body was quite small and still. From what little I had studied of occupational therapy in university, I knew that he must be paralyzed, and my heart reached out to him.

"Yes," I replied to his question, wondering at the same time why this child looked so familiar. He had a sweet, heart-shaped face and an uncontrollable shock of dark hair that stood up from his forehead, giving him a surprised, impish look.

"Did you come on a plane?" he asked. The woman, whom I took to be his nurse or nanny, shifted uncomfortably as if she wanted to go, but clearly the child had other things in mind.

"That's right," I replied to his question.

"Was it a long way?" the child persisted.

"All the way from New York!"

He looked thoughtful for a few seconds. "I went to New York once," he said finally, with a troubled look. "That's where I went for my operation."

"Don't think about that, it will only upset you," interrupted the woman as she started to move the wheelchair. Her concern for him seemed genuine, but she obviously wanted to move him away from me.

The boy paid no attention. "But I want to talk to the lady, Mauricia!" He turned to me. "What's your name?"

"Vivian. What's yours?"

"Harold. Do you know that this island once belonged to the British? Some of my family were English."

"I know that the British occupied most of the islands in the Caribbean," I replied. Then, not wanting to seem too pedantic, I added, "I like your name, Harold."

"Everyone calls me Skip," he replied.

I thought it ironic that he should have such a nickname. Skipping was something he would never do—*might* never do, I corrected myself, thinking of my initial training as an occupational therapist. I guessed he'd been named Skip before he became paralyzed, and I wondered what had caused such a sad disability. But in spite of his injury, he seemed to be a cheerful, very chipper little guy.

"Would it be all right if I called you Skip, too?" I asked.

"Yes," he replied a little pompously, in a way that made me smile. "I will allow you to do that."

He had big dark eyes that seemed to take in everything. He looked at me for a minute, noticing that I was staring at the flower he held in his pale, delicate hands. "Do you like it?" he asked.

"It's beautiful! It almost looks as though it were made of porcelain."

He hooted with laughter. "That's exactly what it's called! A porcelain rose! Would you like to have it?"

"What a lovely gift!"

"You'll have to take it out of my hand. I can't move my arm."

Pain stabbed at my heart. I reached down to take the flower very gently and raised it to my cheek. "Thank you, Skip."

Impatiently, Mauricia gave the wheelchair a little push. "We must go back to the house, Skip. Doctor Michael will be coming soon."

"Wait! I'm not finished!" he shot back. He turned to look at me. "Do you know how to play dominoes?"

"Yes," I replied.

"Good. Then you come with us."

The governess shook her head. "That's not a good idea," she protested.

"Why not?" argued the boy, obviously irritated. "I want her to come! Besides, you don't know how to play dominoes...."

I hesitated.

"Please, Vivian!" he implored, starting to cry.

"Don't cry," Mauricia said to him gently. "You know how your father and I hate to see you cry!"

She turned to me. "I'm afraid he might only get upset.

And then there will be no way to console him.... "

"Perhaps I shouldn't come, although I'd love to," I said to Skip, trying to explain. "Some other time, maybe."

"Of course you should come...now!" insisted Skip, his eyes filling with tears. "I want you to come now!"

"All right," Mauricia finally agreed. "But when Doctor Michael comes, you'll have to go," she said, turning to me.

"Come during siesta. That's soon," suggested Skip, obviously feeling a little more reassured. "I hate siesta! Everyone else goes to sleep and I'm left all by myself."

Still uncertain, I waited for the governess to approve.

"Yes, madam," she said flatly. "That might be the best time for you to come. Harold's room is next to Mr. de Vergoff's study. Do you know how to find it?"

"Yes," I replied, hoping she didn't notice that I was flustered and blushing. I remembered the toys and child's things in the room in which I hid when I was following James de Vergoff. That must have been Skip's room.

"Promise you'll come!" insisted the little boy.

"I promise."

"Cross your heart?"

"Cross my heart!"

I stood watching while Mauricia turned the wheelchair and slowly pushed it back to the house. With feelings that were mixed and more than a little confused, I continued my walk.

The child had touched me deeply. It wasn't easy to grow up within the confines of a wheelchair. Yet he seemed to maintain a very positive and cheerful attitude toward life.

A turn in the path brought me suddenly to a lookout point, from which I could see the entire island. Eagerly I tried to get my bearings. From what I could see, which was quite a lot, I was on a fairly small island. It wouldn't be im-

possible to walk from one end to the other in a day, except
for the steep mountain on the far side. Judging from its
shape and the lack of foliage at its peak, I wondered if it
might be a volcano. I noticed that wisps of cloud or smoke
drifted up from its center and I wondered if it was still active, as some Caribbean volcanoes were.

Then I noticed that there were a number of huts built on
the side of the mountain. If it were indeed a volcano, it
couldn't possibly be active. Circling the island were gleaming white beaches, spotted here and there with fishermen's
huts. The sea, of course, seemed to go on forever. On the
distant horizon I could barely make out what might be
another island—although it was so distant and vague, it
could have been only a rain cloud.

Nothing I could see promised any means of escape, except for the very insecure-looking, tiny fishermen's boats. I
wondered where the airstrip was, and where the large supply boats would dock. They would have to be either on the
far side of the mountain or behind me, on the other side of
the house. Perhaps I could persuade a local fisherman to
take me to another island. But for that I would have to
have money, which I was entirely without. I was also without any identification, or a passport. What would I do if I
did get to another island? Without money, a passport or
any identification, I would probably end up in jail...or
worse.

It occured to me that I could call Sandra, collect. Surely
she would be able to wire me some money—perhaps even
fly down to rescue me and bring me my identification and
passport. If, that is, she could get my things from Martin's
house. If Martin were in on this outrageous scheme, he certainly wouldn't allow her to rescue me.

But no matter what, I realized that I would need money, or some form of barter. That would take some thought and planning.

I glanced at my watch. It was probably siesta time now. I remembered my promise to little Skip and decided I'd better call it a day for sleuthing. Escaping from kidnappers might be important, but nothing could be more important than keeping a promise to a crippled child. I turned and started back to the house.

IT WAS LATE AFTERNOON and the old house was completely silent. Everyone was taking a siesta. I went into the house and through to the area where the study was, then knocked on the door to the room in which I had hidden while James deVergoff was in his study down the hall. My assumption that this room was Skip's turned out to be correct.

"Come in!" called a small voice that could be barely heard through the door.

I walked into the room. Stretched out on a chaise longue, Skip greeted me with a smile. Holding a finger to his lips, he moved his eyes to the figure lying on a couch and then looked back to me. It was Mauricia, sound asleep, her mouth open and her bandanna slightly askew.

"Everything's ready," whispered Skip. "Let's play dominoes!"

Next to his chair a game of dominoes had been set up on a small table covered with a white tablecloth. A wicker chair had been placed on the other side of the table, facing Skip.

"I was afraid you wouldn't come," whispered the little boy, making an awkward movement with his arm toward my left hand. His other arm seemed quite immobile.

Even the arm that he used seemed restricted in movement, except for the fingers on his hand. From the wrist up, it was propped against a cushion at the boy's side.

"Who's your friend?" I whispered, indicating the small animal crouched on his shoulder.

"Chin Chin, my monkey."

The little monkey was concentrating on the banana he was carefully peeling with tiny wrinkled hands that seemed remarkably human. His long tail was wrapped securely around Skip's neck.

"Go on, now, Chin Chin," ordered the boy. "Back to your swing!"

Absorbed in his preoccupation, the monkey made no move to obey.

"Would you take him?" asked Skip. "If he isn't put on his swing, he'll stick to me like glue."

I reached over to pick up the monkey and found the task wasn't as easy as it looked. With his tail, the little creature clung to the boy's neck with such strength that only with a good deal of effort was I able to pull it free. I wondered a little at the risk of leaving an animal with such power clinging to the neck of a little boy whose handicap rendered him practically helpless. With Mauricia sound asleep, anything might have happened.

"He certainly wraps his tail around your neck, doesn't he?" I asked. "Doesn't it hurt?"

"Sometimes," the boy replied indifferently. "Chin Chin can be very stubborn, you know."

I promised myself to speak to Christine. Perhaps she could do something about it—she had said she was in control of everything that went on in the household. It certainly wasn't a safe situation for the helpless young boy.

I sat down on the chair opposite Skip and we started our

game of dominoes. He showed real animation as he became more and more interested in the game. I watched his joy with pleasure. Was he James deVergoff's son? How had he become paralyzed? Where was his mother...other members of his family? I wanted to ask the child these questions, but wisely I bit my tongue. I was afraid that until I knew more, I might risk upsetting Skip. So we played enthusiastically in silence for a period of time, whispering our playful comments back and forth to each other. Of course, I let Skip win the first game. After that, I won the next two games.

Skip was challenging me to another when the door behind me opened.

I turned quickly and saw the tall figure of James deVergoff coming into the room. He stopped in his tracks when he saw me. I got up from my chair.

He was wearing a khaki suit and a pair of sunglasses that hid his eyes. He cut an imposing figure in the doorway.

In spite of myself, I was terrified. The memory of helplessness in the hands of my abductor swept over me. I started feeling faint and weak in the knees, and I knew that I had to get out before I fainted. But to do that I would have to pass James deVergoff. I had no choice; I had no intention of being trapped in the same room with the man who was my kidnapper.

Without saying anything, I hurried across the room to the door and started to push my way through.

"Vivian!" Skip called out. "Don't go away!"

Skip's cry caused Mauricia to stir in her sleep.

"Just a minute!" protested the plantation owner quietly, putting his hand out to stop me.

I didn't hesitate more than a second. I pushed past him. His touch was warm and gentle, unlike my memory of cold, hard hands the night I was taken. I looked up at him. His dark, handsome face expressed concern. He smiled, an open, warmhearted smile that was hard to suspect. How could I fear this man, I thought, and my heart softened briefly. But the memory of the previous night overwhelmed me. Faint with terror, I kept right on going. My heart racing, I didn't stop until I had reached the protective seclusion of my room.

Chapter 7

With relief, I closed the door to my room behind me. I leaned back against the door, closing my eyes, catching my breath. I was beginning to feel that I would collapse under the strain. James deVergoff seemed so different to me this time...so unthreatening.

I jumped at the sound of knocking on the door behind me. I thought it must have been James deVergoff following me. I wondered if I should open the door.

"Who is it?" I asked, unable to keep my voice from trembling.

"Lucille, madam," a soft, quiet voice answered.

I laughed. Poor Lucille. I didn't know who was more frightened. What a sad state of affairs.

I opened the door. Lucille looked as uncomfortable as ever, laden with a tray piled high with a variety of steaming and fragrant dishes. As if this weren't enough, under her arm she held a number of newspapers, their angle suggesting they would slip at any second.

"Watch out! It looks like you might lose something!" I exclaimed, rushing to her aid and taking the papers.

"Oh, madam, thank you." She smiled, a bit more at ease. Evidently I wasn't as much of a monster as she had imagined me to be.

"You're carrying quite a load there," I laughed, putting the papers down. "Now, can I take the tray, as well?"

"No, madam, that's all right. I'll put it on the table here, thank you," she replied, her voice lilting with the musical sound of the local accent. "I hope you like the dinner tonight—it's shrimp creole. Let me know if there's anything more you need," she added, backing gracefully out the doorway.

"Oh, you asked about Madam Christine," she added, turning as she was leaving. "She said that she'll see you in the morning. Today she is busy with household affairs. She said she trusts that that will be all right with you and that all your needs are taken care of."

"That's fine, Lucille," I answered. I wasn't disappointed; I could use a rest for the remainder of the day.

Judging from the aroma filling the room, the dinner would be delicious. Suddenly I realized that I was very hungry. I took the plates of food off the tray and arranged them on the table by the open window. It was only after I had everything to my liking and had settled down to an enjoyable and relaxing meal that I glanced at the newspapers Lucille had brought.

It was with quite a start that I discovered they were recent issues of my husband's publications. Why had these been brought to me, I thought as I eagerly opened them.

They had a strange effect on me. It was as though a kind of buoy had suddenly surfaced, somehow connecting me to a world I thought I had left behind. Undoubtedly, the mail had arrived. I remembered hearing a plane overhead and assumed that it had landed on a strip somewhere out of sight of the house.

I considered it quite thoughtful, if strange, of James deVergoff to have the papers delivered to me. I looked through them all with great curiosity. It seemed a long time since I had left New York. And yet it had been only yesterday.

Nowhere could I find any mention of my disappearance. My husband's editorials seemed to be dealing only with the problems of the Third World.

Finally I found the column written by Sandra that had been devoted to the party. I smiled with affection and annoyance when I read about Count Perrin's misconduct. So she had been unable to resist using that bit of information! Of course, nothing of our own conversation was mentioned. Sandra knew where to draw the line.

I recognized a picture of myself taken at the party. Standing next to me was Martin and we were both smiling as we talked with the Italian minister and his wife.

How far away it seemed! How artificial! The life I was experiencing now seemed much more real—and a thousand times more interesting, if frightening. I had lost the sense of boredom that had been paralyzing me in New York, I realized with a laugh.

When I had finished going through the newspapers and magazines, I tossed them onto the sofa. They merely confirmed what I had expected: my husband hadn't been at all alarmed by my disappearance. Having read my farewell note, he had had little reason to go looking for me. Had James deVergoff sent a ransom note? Or was my husband one of the kidnappers? Either way, it seemed that Martin was simply letting things go, waiting. But for what? In any.

case I was quite sure he must have been very resentful toward me for having left him and was probably planning all sorts of punishment that would be waiting for me upon my reappearance.

With such fitful thoughts, I slept very little that night. Certainly it was not the rest I needed. I kept having frightening, horrible dreams of the various phases of my kidnapping...the aggression at the gate, the invisible hands covering my mouth, the odor that hampered my breathing. Having been drugged, I scarcely realized that I was being put into a car. And it was James who had carried out the kidnapping.

THE FOLLOWING MORNING, Christine brought breakfast to me on a tray. "Good morning!" she greeted me at the door. "Are you feeling better?" she asked, as if I were a patient and she a nurse. I was reminded of this mythical medical condition that she claimed I had.

"There's nothing wrong with me that freedom from this island wouldn't cure," I retorted, trying to appear matter-of-fact and not emotional. I would have succeeded better had I not been kept awake most of the night with frightening recollections of my abduction.

"Oh, oh," Christine whispered, playfully backing away from me. "I was only asking," she laughed.

Her infectious good humor was getting the better of me and I joined in with her laughter.

"How would you like to come to the market with me this morning?" she asked. "I generally go into the village on Monday, and I wondered if you might like to get out of the house . . . . Do some sightseeing, if you could call it that. There isn't all that much to see."

"Are you following instructions?" I asked playfully. In

truth, I was surprised that she was encouraging me to continue in my own explorations. What kind of kidnapping operation was this, anyway?

"Well, sort of. Doctor Michael thought that you might be bored. Going to the market might provide a little distraction."

Doctor Michael? I was surprised. I had been expecting her to say that James deVergoff had given her instructions.

"What time do you want to leave?" I asked. It occurred to me that going into the village might prove very useful. I decided that maybe it was going to be my lucky day.

"Ten o'clock," she replied with a happy smile.

It was only eight o'clock, but everyone on the island was up and busy. Activities on the plantation were pretty much regulated by the temperature, it seemed. People started to work early in the morning when it was cool and then rested in the heat of the day.

Before leaving, I wanted to say hello to my young friend, Skip. As soon as I had had breakfast, I went to his room. He was very happy to see me. A woman in a white uniform was leaning over him.

"This is my nurse," announced Skip, by way of introduction.

The woman asked who I was.

"A friend," replied Skip with a smile. "Her name is Vivian and I can beat her at dominoes!"

His answer made it possible for me to avoid any further explanation.

"I'm Judith Aman," stated the woman. "I'm here to see if this young man has been doing his exercises regularly."

"Oh, I don't like doing them," said Skip with a scowl. "What's the use, anyway? The doctors in New York have already told me that I'll never walk again."

"Hogwash!" exclaimed the nurse. "American doctors don't know half as much as they think they do!" Then she straightened up with a sigh. "Come on, Skip. You have to make an effort, you know."

Mauricia was standing at the foot of the bed looking very disapproving. She glanced back and forth from me to the nurse with hostility in her eyes. "Please. Don't ask him to do the impossible," she implored.

"What would you like me to bring you from the market?" I asked the little boy.

"Bring me a surprise!"

At that moment I was reminded of the fact that I had no money to buy anything. I recalled my thoughts on this subject the day before. If I was going to escape, I had to have money. But it bothered me more that I couldn't even buy Skip a simple gift.

I left the room at the same time as the nurse and questioned her in the hallway about the condition of her young patient.

"Is it true that he'll never walk again? Is there no hope?"

"None, unfortunately. But I believe his general condition might be improved considerably. The trouble is he has to be encouraged to start a rehabilitation program and then have the courage to stick with it. His father refuses to make him do anything that might make him cry, and Mauricia, of course, treats him like a baby."

I thought of my brother, Simon, who had had a similar condition, and of what had happened to him.

"Oh, well," sighed the nurse. "They may be right. At any rate, the boy is a cripple and will be one for the rest of his life."

I recalled having heard those pessimistic words before from someone else's mouth. . . .

Our conversation was interrupted by Christine. "Ready?" she called out from the doorway.

"Soon," I answered. "I want to get something from my room first."

Christine was casually and comfortably dressed in shorts and a halter top. *What a pleasant job she has,* I thought to myself as I returned to my room. She could spend her days and nights in an atmosphere of ease and comfort. Here on the island there were no problems; all one had to do was learn how to let go, how to live with a kind of primitive happiness. Life on the island seemed so simple! There appeared to be no need for money. All one needed was a dress and a bathing suit. An abundance of food grew on the island and all around was natural beauty of spectacular proportions.

Christine drove a light truck out of the garage. It had a canvas top that provided protection from the heat of the sun for the driver and passengers. As we drove toward the village, she filled me in on some of the details about the island. The plantation was known as The Mills, deriving its name from the numerous water mills on the property. The island was called St. Victor, and was in the middle of the Caribbean. The produce of the plantation consisted mainly of sugar and bananas. Except for some mountainous parts, the terrain was basically level, and I could have gone to the village on foot. In truth, there were very few cars on the island—the native people moved around in small carts pulled by donkeys. There were no great distances to be travelled; I learned that the island was some seven miles long and only three miles wide.

There were no trains, no traffic jams, no pollution, Christine explained. It all added up to making St. Victor an island paradise, far from the ills of so-called civilization. I had to agree. How fortunate I had been to be kidnapped and brought to this Eden, I thought with a laugh.

Reminded of the fact that I had, indeed, been kidnapped, I was mindful of one of my purposes in going to the village with Christine.

"Is there a pawnshop in the village where I might be able to sell some jewelry?" I asked.

I had already made sure that I still had the pearl necklace, earrings and bracelet that I was wearing the night of the kidnapping. I had found them intact in a small silver box on my night table. Just before leaving for the market I had slipped them into a small purse. They were all I had left of the gifts Martin had given me; I had previously sold the rest and deposited the money in a private bank account. However, my bank was in New York and I had no way of getting hold of the money.

Christine was looking at me strangely. "A pawnshop? You won't find anything like that on this island. But there is a small shop near the market that sells glassware, knick-knacks, this and that.... The owner also has the grocery store. He might be able to do something for you, as long as whatever you want to sell isn't of any great value. The natives here have little money to buy jewelry. However, there are the doctors and their families. Also some marine engineers. Maybe they would be interested."

I showed her what I had.

"Those are real!" she exclaimed as soon as she saw the necklace. "You're not going to sell that? You'll never get the price you should. Doesn't it bother you, getting rid of them?"

"No," I replied firmly. "They have no sentimental value for me at all...." My vague gesture terminated the statement.

I also showed her my wedding band, studded with diamonds. "What about this?" I asked.

"But that's your wedding ring!"

"I don't care much about it, either."

"It must be worth a lot of money," said my companion, her eyes wide with admiration.

"Listen," I said, "I have to have some cash to buy a few things. I want to buy some native handicrafts, and some of the handwoven material.... Actually, I'd like to be able to pick up whatever I might find interesting at the market."

"All right," replied Christine. "We'll go to the shop I was telling you about and see what the owner has to say."

I was enchanted by the marketplace. It was colorful and picturesque. Beneath the multicolored awnings were all kinds of fruit...bananas, mangoes, pineapples. The variety was incredible. Coconuts were piled in huge pyramids and I saw some potatoes that were formed into curious shapes.

"We call that the fruit of the bread tree," explained Christine. "It can be prepared in the same way as potatoes. You know, mashed...fried...whatever."

A fisherman was selling live tortoises with very primitive designs on their shells. "They're sea tortoises," explained Christine, "but they also live on land."

"Do you think Skip would like to have one?" I asked.

"I'm sure he would!" she replied. "I don't suppose anyone has ever thought of getting him one. It's such a little thing. His father gives him extravagant gifts, but he's too preoccupied to give much thought to what the boy might really want to have."

"Then I'll just have to get myself some cash so I can buy one for him," I said.

Christine guided me to a corner of the marketplace,

where we went down two steps into a shop that was cluttered with all kinds of items—canned goods, bottles of rum, gallon containers of syrup and materials in a multitude of colors. Men and women in colorful costumes rummaged through everything. The shopkeeper, his eyes sparkling, greeted us with great enthusiasm. The smile, however, went no further than his lips. I could see the glint in his eyes when I showed him my jewelry.

"You say you want to sell this?" he asked, his eyebrows raised.

"Yes," I replied.

Regretfully, he pushed aside the necklace and then the bracelet. But he took a little more time to examine the ring. Then, with a sad nod of his head, he gave the whole lot back to me. "I'm afraid I wouldn't be able to find a customer for anything like this," he said.

"Perhaps I could leave them here on consignment," I suggested.

He looked dubious but I persisted. "If I were to leave them here, do you think you could give me some credit?"

"A loan?" he queried, looking even more dubious.

"Yes," I answered emphatically.

"How much do you need?" he asked.

I glanced nervously toward Christine. "Oh, four hundred...five hundred dollars." I tried to sound matter-of-fact about it.

Christine looked at me with surprise. There would be no ordinary reason for me to need so much spending money on the island. Certainly, whatever gift I bought for Skip would cost only pennies. Why else would I want so much money?

The shopkeeper thought for a minute. "And you'd be leaving all three items?"

"Of course!"

I could almost see the wheels turning in his head as he made a rapid calculation. "There's just a slight possibility that I might be able to sell one of them," he said finally with an oblique glance toward Christine, who was nudging me with her elbow to stop me from agreeing too quickly. I was relieved that her main concern was that I would lose money on the exchange of my jewels. "There might be someone among the engineers' or doctors' wives who would be interested," the shopkeeper went on.

"All right," Christine agreed. "But make sure you get a good price," she told him firmly. "We don't want to give the gems away."

"I understand completely," gloated the shopkeeper. "It's the only way I do business." He turned to the cash register and counted out some money. "Unfortunately, all I can give you is forty-five dollars," he said. "It's the best I can do."

"Forty-five dollars! Is that all?" I asked imploringly.

The look on his face told me that he would stand firm.

"But the ring itself is worth five thousand!"

"If you prefer, I'll give you forty-five for the ring alone. This isn't a big city, you know. What do you expect? Five dollars is a lot of money to the people here, and forty-five dollars is a fortune. That's all I can offer."

"Agreed," I said abruptly. I couldn't stand not having any money at all. This small amount wouldn't buy my escape off the island, but at least I would be able to entertain myself by buying some things while I was there.

"Don't forget your receipt," cautioned Christine.

As we were leaving the shop she explained that the shopkeeper knew her very well. "He knows that I work for James deVergoff," she remarked. "And I'm sure he realizes that you're part of the household. He wouldn't do anything to cross us—or to jeopardize his own position, for that matter. Just the same, a receipt is always a good idea."

I was feeling much more relaxed now that I had a little money. We made our way back to the marketplace and I felt wonderful knowing that now I was in a position to do some buying. When I admired some yardage, Christine offered me the use of her sewing maching. Before I married I had enjoyed making my own clothes, and the thought of making something for myself out of beautiful cotton fabrics displayed there excited me. If I was going to be a prisoner, I might as well make myself at home, I thought. So I bought some bright, colorful material in an unusual design, thinking it would make a lovely dress.

Then I hurried to the stall where the fisherman was selling his sea turtles. I bought a small one for Skip and the man put it in a gold box, for which he charged extra.

I felt very pleased with myself. I had made several purchases and yet spent very little cash. Inflation, it seemed, was still unknown in that island paradise.

As Christine and I crossed the street to go back to the area where she had parked the panel truck, we encountered James deVergoff in his jeep. He was intent on his destination, his gaze riveted to the road.

"He seems to be everywhere," murmured Christine. "He has an incredible capacity for work. They say he's been like this ever since his wife died. You'd almost think that he hates to be in the house. If it weren't for his son, I don't suppose we'd ever see him."

So Skip was James deVergoff's son, as I had expected. Suddenly I knew why I felt that I'd seen Skip before. I recalled the photograph on the desk in James deVergoff's study that showed a woman with a young boy. And if that boy was Skip, then the woman must have been James deVergoff's wife. . . .

"Oh, I'm sorry to hear that," I said. "I didn't know . . . ."

"That his wife died?"

"Yes." It was a shock, and it pained me to recall her vibrant, happy face. She looked like a woman who had loved life very much. "Did you know his wife?" I asked.

"Catherine? No. My husband's only been the manager here for the past two years. He had a similar position in Jamaica, but it wasn't as important as the one here. Mr. deVergoff hired me to run the household. After his wife died, there seemed to be a constant turnover of servants. Running a house isn't very much different from managing a business; someone has to be in charge to keep things moving smoothly. I understand that everyone here loved Mrs. deVergoff very much. At first, that made things a little difficult for me; it was a while before I was accepted. But when Michael came, things went a little easier."

"Who's Michael?" I asked in innocence.

"Oh . . . you don't know? James's brother, the doctor," Christine explained, speeding the truck to pass a native pulling a cart on the road. She waved and smiled at the man as she passed. "That's Dominique—he's a fisherman. His family lives in the village . . . terrific people. . . . Say, would you like to tour the island? There's no rush to get back, is there?"

I nodded silently. I wasn't paying too much attention to what Christine was saying. Instead, I was putting several pieces of the puzzle together. The Doctor Michael everyone had been mentioning now and then must be this very Michael—James deVergoff's brother.

"But you must know about Michael," Christine continued. "After all, he's why you are here."

"What do you mean?" I asked, trying to sound casual. Inside, of course, I was racing to hear what information she might have to offer.

"Michael is a world-famous doctor. Your husband sent you here to have a rest, no doubt, but also to be under his care. You're fortunate, really. He doesn't have much time for patients these days. He's too busy setting up a hospital here and on other islands as well as helping James run The Mills."

I was speechless with surprise. Christine, I was sure, thought that what she was saying was the truth. I couldn't possibly doubt her; she spoke with such open candor. If she only knew how brutally I'd been transported! It certainly wasn't the caring expression of husbandly love and concern that she envisioned.

"Who told you the reason for my being here?" I asked.

"Why, James, of course," she answered, looking at me as if to say that she thought my question was an odd one.

I wondered if Michael deVergoff was involved in the kidnapping as well. "James and Michael work together, do they?" I continued, again trying to make my question seem an ordinary one.

"Oh, yes, in every way. They're very close. Michael came to the island after James's wife died to look after Harold—or Skip, as we call him—and to help James with the running of the plantation. I guess James took his wife's death pretty hard, because it was a while before things were back to normal around here."

"Do they share the responsibilities equally?" I inquired.

"I suppose you could say that, although they do different things. James deVergoff is what you might call the 'big boss' on the island, but his brother has taken over the matters that concern the plantation but have to be dealt with elsewhere. He handles most of the commercial transactions and public relations, negotiates contracts, deals with the customers, that sort of thing. He spends quite a bit of time traveling abroad. He has a pilot's license and flies his own plane."

"James deVergoff doesn't fly?"

"Oh, he did before his wife died, I understand. And lately he's started making the occasional trip. But usually he stays on the island," she concluded.

I had been wondering how my kidnapping could have been accomplished in such absolute secrecy. I didn't have to wonder anymore. Michael deVergoff must have flown the plane that brought me here. How else would they have brought the unconscious body of an unidentified woman across international boundaries without question? Something like that could only be accomplished in a private plane. So both Michael and James were in on the kidnapping.

"By the way," I asked, "is there any kind of regular service to and from the island?"

"Not officially," replied Christine. "The island is privately owned, of course, which means that the airport and landing strip are not available for use by commercial airlines unless special permission is given."

"Then how do people get here? They must have some visitors, surely. And what about customers and suppliers? Don't the people who live on the island ever travel?"

"Sometimes, but usually they go by boat. The fishermen come and go between the various islands of the archipelago where people can get a flight on one of the regular airlines. But most of the time, when a customer or family friend or even doctor or technician comes to the plantation, Michael deVergoff will pick him up and fly him here in the company plane."

"What about the mail?"

"It's the same sort of thing. Either Michael picks it up from one of the other islands, or the service boat goes and gets it. The tobacco exchange here doubles as a post office."

"Well," I concluded. "These gentlemen certainly do everything possible to protect their little empire from the outside world!"

"That's right," agreed Christine. "They're very much the masters of their domain. You won't find just anyone coming here! It seems that things were quite different while Mrs. deVergoff was still alive," Christine went on. "There were lavish parties and lots of company on the island much of the time. Catherine was very happy and full of life; she was forever inviting people to come and stay here. Well, all that changed when she died. James turned away from any kind of social activity, and the house is a very sad place now. Michael is the only one who ever brings anyone here. He has a few friends and they play tennis together and go for cruises on his yacht. But even that doesn't amount to much. James simply doesn't want to have anyone around."

We were crossing through banana tree orchards, their limbs laden with layered stacks of the heavy fruit.

"Does Michael deVergoff live here?" I inquired. "I haven't seen him. He must have family...children.... Is he married?"

"No," replied Christine with a shake of her head. "He lives here, but he lives alone. He spends most of his time at the hospital or traveling. In fact, I've never seen him with a woman." She laughed and looked at me shyly. "Well, you know the type.... I expect he has a woman in every port, as the saying goes. I'm sure he has all sorts of things going for him elsewhere, but we don't hear anything about it here. At least, I haven't heard any gossip since I've been here!"

We continued in silence for a moment. Then Christine decided she would like to try to find her husband, who was working somewhere on the plantation. "Just to say hello," she explained with a smile. "We've got lots of time. The men have lunch at the rum distillery, so we don't have to worry about keeping any schedule."

The suggestion was fine with me. I hadn't had much chance to see the plantation and was glad to have an opportunity to do so. The weather was perfect. The more we traveled around, the more I became convinced that the island was indeed some kind of paradise, an expression often misused, but in this case very apt. The tropical atmosphere and Christine's relaxed company put me entirely at ease. Slowly, I was putting aside my suspicious thoughts and tormented searching.

The old truck chugged along unpaved side roads between fields of sugarcane and banana orchards. Christine explained that the white arrows above the canes signified that it was time for the harvest.

Further on there were fields of pineapple and we passed by old mills, relics of years gone by. From time to time we came upon a communal laundry set alongside the roadway and heard the echo of the native people singing as they did their washing. The women looked up to wave and smile a greeting as we drove by.

We passed in front of the rum distillery, which was also known as the hospitality house because one of its wings was reserved for distinguished guests, Christine explained.

Finally we arrived at the sugar mill where Christine's husband was working. It was a large building in which the cane was processed. Bundles of cane were piled high everywhere. The earth had been badly torn up by the trucks coming and going, transporting the sugarcane from the fields, and we had to cross quite a large area of muddy terrain to reach the door of the mill. I could hear the noise of the machinery inside. Finally I was going to see something of the industry of the plantation.

Christine called out and a tall, bare-chested black man came out of the building, his moist face wreathed in a wide smile. He ran to us and apologized for his appearance. "I've been working on the crusher," he explained.

He made a move toward Christine, who quickly put her hands up in front of her. "Oh, no you don't," she laughed. "No hugs, Theodore! You're soaking wet!"

He threw his head back and laughed heartily. "You'd be perspiring too, if you had to work on that damn machine! What are you doing here, anyway?"

Christine explained that we had simply dropped by on our way back to the house after a trip to the marketplace. Her husband just kept on smiling and leaned forward to give Christine a slight slap on the bottom.

He took us into what appeared to be a coffee shop that obviously served as a lunchroom and recreation area for the workers. There was a pool table, a Ping-Pong table and any number of decks of cards, as well as eating tables. Air conditioning made the room quite comfortable. Theodore got us a rum punch that was very refreshing and later accompanied us back to the truck. He explained that we were on the north section of the island, which was surrounded by mountains.

"Look over there," he said, pointing to a peak shrouded in cloud. "That's the Tilsun volcano."

Down the slope of the mountainside I could see the red tile roofs of native houses. "Aren't the people afraid of the volcano?" I asked in surprise.

"There hasn't been an eruption for a long time. As a matter of fact, I've never even heard anyone talking about it," he replied.

"How do the people live on that part of the island?"

"They cultivate the land. And they raise animals, fruit trees. They even grow grapes up there."

"And how are the children educated?" I persisted.

"They have their own school. It's at the foot of the hill next to the church. Look, you can see it from here.... You really should try to visit it, you know. It's one of the oldest in all of the Caribbean."

When the manager had seen us to the truck and left, Christine turned to me with a smile. "Well, what did you think of him?"

"Your husband? He seems very nice," I replied.

"He's from Guadeloupe originally. I met him in the States where he was attending the Institute of Agriculture. I was taking a course in hotel management at the time. We've been married four years."

She was positively radiant. "I love him," she went on softly. "And he can't get along without me. We're very happy."

"Do you have any children?" I asked softly, moved by her obvious and deep contentment in her marriage.

Her face became quite serious. "Not yet," she said. "We're waiting until our financial position gets a little better."

She hesitated for a moment, lost in thought, before continuing. I waited.

"When we have enough money," she said, her eyes shining, "we're going to buy a hotel in the Caribbean. In the meantime, neither of us can imagine living anywhere else. We love it here. Maybe we will stay."

"Have you thought about starting up a business here, on St. Victor Island?" I asked.

"Not really. The way things are now, the island isn't open to tourists. And who knows whether the deVergoff brothers might ever decide to change that? I kind of hope they don't—it's so beautiful the way it is. Tourists always spoil things a little bit."

"Yes." I nodded in agreement, but my thoughts were elsewhere. I was thinking about Christine's radiant happiness, her love for her husband, their plans for their future together. I envied her terribly. For all the wealth I had known, I had missed the only really important thing in life—love. Without it, even the most splendid castle seems bare. I wondered, sadly, if I would ever know the loving happiness that was Christine's.

Chapter 8

When we got back, I went straight to Skip's room. I was eager to see if he would like the gift I had bought him. He was delighted with it. He put it on the table next to him where he kept his favorite toys and asked Mauricia to bring a bowl of water so that the tortoise could have a swim. His pet monkey looked with curiosity at the strange little creature.

"I hope the two of you are going to get along together," said Skip to the monkey. He turned to me. "I'm going to call her Flippers," he announced.

"Why Flippers?"

"Because it suits her," he replied, very satisfied with his choice.

I spent most of the afternoon with the crippled child; while I was with him, I could forget all the things that were bothering me. But I couldn't help wondering what James's reaction would be when the plan he had so carefully worked out would not bring the results he was seeking. Time seemed to be dragging by. I knew it wouldn't be long before he found out; Martin's silence would soon become very conspicuous. What would James do?

Thoughts like these constantly disturbed my peace of mind. Otherwise, I felt perfectly serene in the island setting. I couldn't remember ever having been quite so comfortable before. I was starting to feel less and less anxious about escape. More and more, I found myself postponing whatever efforts I could make in that direction. Also, already I was growing quite fond of Christine and especially Skip. I didn't want to simply disappear from their lives without a trace.

I sat down in the chair next to Skip. "Would you like me to tell you a story, young man?"

"Oh, yes! I love stories!"

He was looking at me with his huge, sad eyes, set deep in his small face. They were softer and more melancholy than any eyes I had ever seen. I wondered if he had his mother's eyes. Perhaps all the joy and happiness had gone from his life at the time of the accident.

"Well, where's my story?" insisted the little boy impatiently.

"It's the story of a boy about your age. Actually, he was just five. He was full of life and loved to run and jump. I think the thing he liked to do best was climb trees."

Skip was hanging on my every word.

Mauricia, who'd been sitting quietly on the sofa, suddenly interrupted sharply. "What are you telling him? You're only going to hurt him, you know! He can hardly move! How can you tell him such stories?"

"We all know that, Mauricia," Skip interrupted with an understanding beyond his years. "But it's okay. Please, let

Vivian tell me the story. I like it! And I like the little boy.... By the way, what was his name?"

"Simon," I replied, and went on with my story despite Mauricia's obvious disapproval. "One day," I continued, "the little boy was very careless and fell to the ground from the highest branch of a huge oak tree."

"Gosh! Was he killed?" Skip's face creased with anxiety.

"No, fortunately he wasn't killed. But he stayed there on the ground for quite a long time, unable to get up. When he finally was found he was stiff as a board. The doctors said that he had damaged his spine and would never walk again."

"Just like me," sighed the little boy.

"What are you trying to do?" intervened Mauricia once more, her voice bitter. "I'm going to tell Mr. deVergoff that you're tormenting the boy!"

"She's not tormenting me at all," argued Skip, his tone revealing irritation. "Please! Let her tell the story!"

Then he turned to me with a worried frown. "Was he really just like me, Vivian? Did he have to sit in a wheelchair?"

"At first he had to lie in bed, facedown," I replied. "He couldn't even move his head. He had to be fed like a little baby and he didn't like any part of it."

"I don't blame him.... What happened to him? What's the end of the story?"

"Well, Skip, it's a happy ending. Three years later, he won a trophy for being the best swimmer in his competition class!"

"Honest?"

"Cross my heart!" I smiled.

"But, how come? Was it a miracle or something?"

"Part miracle, perhaps.... But mostly it was a triumph

of the will. That little boy simply wouldn't accept the doctor's verdict. He just refused to be paralyzed for the rest of his life. And his father, even though he was just a country doctor, did everything he could to help him. Somehow they managed to convince each other that there was hope.

"Now, with only that spark of hope to go on, Simon decided to do something about his condition. Day in and day out, starting slowly and gradually building up, he courageously did his exercises. He put his muscles to work, forced himself to make each movement, even though it was often painful. He just wouldn't give up! He was only five years old, but he fought like a tiger.

"Before very long, all his hard work started to show results. Everyone was astounded! Eventually he was able to stand up. Then he could walk with the help of canes. And finally we put away his hospital bed and his wheelchair once and for all."

Skip was listening to me with his mouth open and his eyes aglow. "Then what?" he demanded.

"Well, now he is able to function pretty much like any normal human being. Except, of course, he can't walk without the help of his canes. But he's so good at it, somehow it doesn't seem to matter very much. He drives a car that has been changed so it can be hand controlled. And, of course, when he wants to travel long distances, he goes by plane. A far cry from being completely paralyzed, right?"

"Do you ever see him?"

I didn't answer right away. I thought of my younger brother and all the things that separated us. Simon had eventually realized the wish formulated while he was fighting his handicap. He had made a vow to devote his life to others and had entered a religious order to become a missionary in Africa. He had completed his medical studies and now was the head of a missionary hospital.

Impatient at my silence, Skip repeated his question.

"No, I don't see him because he lives far away, in another country. But he'll come back one day and then I'll see him," I replied. I could feel my eyes getting moist as I thought of that possibility.

Skip was very thoughtful. It seemed as though my story was having an effect on him. "Do you think I could do what Simon did?"

"I don't know, Skip. I don't know whether your condition is the same as Simon's was. But I do know that you'd have to have a great deal of courage. Overcoming such a handicap is a long, hard struggle."

"But the doctors . . . ."

"Yes, I know. The doctors," I murmured. "Trouble is, some of them don't give enough credit to the human will, especially when the human is a young man of six, like yourself. Your nurse has already told me that you haven't been making any progress because you don't want to do any of the things that are required if you are to be rehabilitated. No one can do it for you, Skip. Nor can anyone else help you until you begin to help yourself."

He looked at me intently. Deep in his sad eyes I thought I could see the beginnings of a small flame. Suddenly his pale face relaxed in a smile. "Oh, I want to get better, Vivian! You don't know how much I want to!"

"Then you'll have to start your exercises right away and stick with them every single day! Agreed?"

"Agreed!" he exclaimed, his face bright. I promised myself that I would do everything I could to help him for as long as I would be around.

Skip and I were just going to start another game of

dominoes when Christine came to the door of the room. "Vivian, Doctor Michael says that he wants to see you soon. Are you free right now?"

I looked with good humor toward Skip, who winked back at me.

"No, she's not free, Christine! She's all mine!" he chirped playfully.

"Well. . .how about after this game?" I ventured.

"Fine. Actually, he wants to see Skip, too, so why don't you just stay here."

"Okay," I replied as calmly as I could. My heart was racing. After so much mystery, I was eager to see who the famous doctor-turned-kidnapper was. And with little Skip with me, I knew I need fear no harm.

But before long we were immersed in a new game. Skip would direct me around the room with instructions of "hot" or "cold," in search of a secret object. My confusion led me into his closet. I could hear Skip squealing with laughter as he cried out "hot," "hot," "hotter still!"

"But it's dark in here!" I protested. "I can't see anything!" My voice, no doubt, was muffled by the hanging clothing, which only delighted Skip all the more.

"Skip! Help! How can I find something if I can't see it?" I called out, this time growing just a bit impatient. "You're trying to fool me!" I said, bursting out of the closet and into the arms of a man.

"What?" I exclaimed in confusion, blinded by the light of the room. I looked up into the laughing face of James deVergoff, and my knees buckled.

"No! No!" I cried out. I started to scream, but I was powerless. Instead, a pathetic cry escaped my lips as I sank to the floor. I couldn't focus; the room was spinning around me and I felt faint.

"Mauricia! Get me some water, quick!" the man exclaimed, catching me in his arms and gently moving me onto the couch. He put me down, slipping a pillow under my feet, and soothingly stroked my forehead and cheeks.

"Oh, I'm sorry," I heard his whisper. "I didn't mean to startle you."

Faintly, as though through a fog, I could hear the sound of a child crying. Skip. . .it must be Skip.

"Don't worry, Skip. Don't cry," I heard James deVergoff say to his son. "She's only fainted. She was surprised to see me, I suppose. She'll be up and about in no time, you'll see."

I struggled to come to consciousness. My head was being moved. I realized that he was lifting my head with one hand and encouraging me to sip from a glass of water Mauricia had brought.

Slowly the fog cleared from my mind. I opened my eyes and looked directly into James deVergoff's crystal blue eyes. His handsome face expressed curiosity and concern. His light blue eyes stood out in contrast to the darkness of his tanned complexion and raven black hair.

But the harsh memory of those very eyes came back to me—their icy, penetrating stare. I remembered the cold, hard clasp of hands binding me and the memory of a man without emotion. I struggled to sit up and flee.

"Is she okay?" I heard the child's voice call out. "She's moving! She's okay!" he exclaimed with obvious joy.

I clung to the thought that I must not frighten Skip, alarm him. I had to bring my emotions under control, if only for his sake.

"What happened?" I asked. "Did I faint?"

"You would have fallen on the floor," Skip cried out excitedly. "I saw!"

"Hi, Skip," I greeted the child. I felt as if I had been away for a long time—not just a few seconds. "Imagine, directing me into the closet!" I said with a laugh, wanting to make light of the situation for his sake.

"To return to your question," James deVergoff said formally, "yes, you did faint. But you'll be just fine. What I want to know is why you fainted. Are you on any medication that I should know about?"

I was surprised by his question. Of course he knew why I had fainted; he just wasn't going to let on.

"No, I'm not on any medication," I answered. "I fainted because you surprised me. Why should I be on any medication?" I added.

"Because of your condition," he answered.

"What condition?" I asked bluntly.

"I'd rather not discuss that in front of the child," he said, nodding toward Skip.

"Why not? I want to know, too!" Skip called out quickly, never missing anything that happened. He wasn't really interested; he only wanted to know about anything that was considered secret.

"Not now, Skip," James told his son. "Mauricia, has Skip had his afternoon snack yet?"

Mauricia gave a negative shake of her head.

"Well, perhaps now would be a good time to give it to him. Why don't you both go to the dining room. I want to talk to Mrs. Fawkes in private for a minute or two."

My heart was beating. I was still weak from having fainted, but the prospect of being alone with this man, without the protective company of another woman and a child, frightened me even more.

"No!" I called out, the urgency in my voice betraying my

emotion. "They can stay, surely. Or, why don't I go with them? I'm hungry, too...."

"There's no need to be frightened, Mrs. Fawkes, I assure you," James deVergoff said gently. "I've been busy and I haven't had a chance to see you, I'm afraid. It's time we had a chat. I'm sorry, but I have to admit that you've been neglected a bit."

"Neglected?" I muttered, confused. I was too puzzled to do anything more than go along with what he wanted.

Mauricia lifted Skip into his wheelchair and wheeled him toward the door.

"Come back in about half an hour, Mauricia. I'll want to give Skip his examination then."

Mauricia nodded and Skip turned his head and waved. "See you later!" he called out with a smile.

"Later!" I waved back, responding to his gesture with a smile of my own. The child had a way of making even my most horrible moments seem light and pleasant.

"He's a wonderful little boy, isn't he?" James deVergoff said after Mauricia had closed the door behind them, leaving the two of us alone together in the room.

"Yes," I answered enthusiastically. "We've become fast friends. I quite adore him."

"The feeling seems to be a mutual one," he noted. "I like to see him happy. His condition is such a tragic one. It concerns me that he doesn't seem to be making any progress.... However, I want to talk about you, not Skip!"

I was growing more and more angry with his casual attitude toward my involuntary imprisonment—my kidnapping. How could he be so offhand about everything? I decided to be blunt and to the point.

"Why did you kidnap me?" I asked aggressively, looking him full in the face. Inside, I was shaking; outside, I hoped that I at least appeared brave and defiant.

"Kidnap you? Christine mentioned to me that you felt you'd been kidnapped. Tell me, have you ever felt that you've been kidnapped before?"

I was enraged. "Of course not! How many times do you think one gets kidnapped in one's life? I've been kidnapped...and by you! You know it and you're the one who is creating fabrications, not me. What do you think I am—crazy?"

"Well...you have had a history of...history of needing hospitalization...."

"Hospitalization? Oh, for having my tonsils removed—do you consider that a 'history' of hospitalization? What I want to know is why you kidnapped me. You haven't answered my question yet." I was furious. No longer was I frightened by my situation; rather, I was fighting mad.

"Please calm down, Mrs. Fawkes. I didn't want to upset you. You're here to rest, to recover...."

"From what? What do you mean, rest? What type of kidnapper are you, anyway? Let's set the record straight. You attack me in my own home, drug me, brutally force me here, and now you're trying to drive me insane by pretending that none of it ever happened, that I simply imagined that I'd been kidnapped. I don't know why you are doing this, but believe me, if I ever get to the bottom of this, if I ever live to see my friends again, I'm going to...."

My anger gave way to sobs I could not control. My frustration had been so great, the mystery surrounding everything on this island so bewildering, that James deVergoff's unexpected response overwhelmed me.

"I can't...I can't," I sobbed. "I just can't...take it anymore."

He studied me. The room was silent except for the sound of my sobs. Even Chin Chin, the monkey, stopped his curious explorations to study me.

"I didn't mean to upset you," James deVergoff ventured hesitantly. I could see that he was baffled by my outburst. He moved beside me on the couch, handed me a tissue and gently put his hand on the back of my neck.

I shuddered at his touch. I was embarrassed. I didn't like losing control, especially in front of him. But now I was only aware of his gentle hand on my neck, his warmth, the strong comfort he was tenderly offering.

He bent over me, brushing my cheek lightly with his lips, pressing me gently toward him, into his caring, protective arms. His fingers played lightly with the hair at the back of my neck, his lips brushing my forehead, my cheeks, moving more and more urgently toward my mouth. *No, no*, I thought, yet I yearned with all my being to embrace him—yearned for one more touch, one more tender, gently stroking kiss. His searching lips found mine, and whatever resistance I had fell away to the pleasure of his touch.

No, I cried out to myself. *This man is your kidnapper!* Abruptly I broke away, weak with emotion. Tears ran down my cheeks as I got to my feet and stumbled out the door.

"Wait! Vivian, please...." James deVergoff called out after me. He started to follow me out the door, but I turned and gave him a beseeching look. I had to get away.

He stopped, respecting my need, and watched me in silence as I climbed the stairs to my room.

Chapter 9

I lay down on my bed and tried to collect my thoughts. Yet the only thing I could think off was James's kiss. Even now, my body was singing to the memory of his touch. I had never been so overwhelmed, had never known that a man could be so gentle, so sensual and enticing.

A wave of shame came over me at the realization what had just happened. My kidnapper—the man who had abducted me, drugged me and held me prisoner—had kissed me and I had welcomed him! I hadn't even protested.

It terrified me to think how little control I had over my emotions. I recalled my hysterical sobbing outburst, my fainting, my terror... and then my passion. I felt helpless. On this island of illusion, where nothing was what it seemed to be, where kidnappers denied that they were kidnappers, what could I count on except myself? And now... now I couldn't even count on myself.

Clearly, I was going to have to take action. So far I had been the victim of James deVergoff's whims and actions. If I was going to survive, I would have to take the first step. It was his turn to be caught off guard, not mine.

I decided to rest and have dinner before I attempted anything. Maybe I would even have a sauna and a long leisurely bath—I deserved one. I rang for Lucille, ordered my dinner, and then prepared my bath. As I sprinkled fragrant oils into the water, I sighed with the luxury of escape. Maybe I would even do some sewing before dinner.

Such were the thoughts I had that served to take my mind off the overwhelming episodes of the day, to prepare me and give me strength for the even more demanding events to come in the evening ahead.

OVER A STEAMING CUP of after-dinner coffee, I thought about what I knew I had to do. I had to get more information, and the only way to do that would be break into James deVergoff's study one more time. There had to be another file that could help explain what was going on...and why.

I planned to go in the very late evening, when everyone was most likely settled down for the night. That way, I would probably not be discovered.

The hours passed slowly. I had a hard time concentrating on my sewing. I found that I made mistakes, joining the wrong pieces of fabric together. Deciding to read, I only discovered that I was reading the same paragraph over and over again, not following the story. Obviously, I was too nervous to do anything.

Finally the sun set. It became dark and the sounds of the animals and birds gradually faded away. Now and then I could hear the sound of a child crying, or laughter, but otherwise all was silent. It was time for me to go.

I slipped out my door, into the hall and down the stairs. All the lights were out and the hallway was quite dark.

I stopped. I thought I heard the sounds of men's voices. It was then that I noticed there was a light shining from under the study door. Trembling with fear, I stepped a bit closer. Yes, the voices were in the study, and from what I could hear, they seemed to be quite angry.

I slipped next to the door and pressed my ear to it, determined to find out what was happening inside.

"How *could* you?" I heard one man exclaim. My heart raced. It was James's voice. "And I thought that I could trust you," he went on, his deep voice expressing disappointment.

"Obviously, you don't understand," said the other man. I guessed that it must be Michael, James's brother.

"What do you mean, *I* don't understand?" James said loudly. "It's *you* who doesn't understand. Don't you know the law? Don't you understand what's going to happen to you because of what you've done? And what will happen to your son, Skip? Have you thought of that?"

His son? But I thought Skip was James's son. I was totally confused, but could only listen as the other man's voice went on.

"There are higher, more important laws. Skip will be looked after, as will we all."

There was a very long silence.

"I see," I heard James say slowly.

Then the sound of footsteps coming toward the door sent me running down the hall to another room. The study door opened and I saw James stride quickly down the hall.

I stood in silence, thinking. So it was Michael who had

kidnapped me. Why? I had to know, and I knew that there was only one way I would ever find out: by asking the kidnapper.

With a brave spirit I didn't know I had, I stepped up to the door and knocked.

"Come in!" The voice was crisp and emotionless.

I opened the door and walked in. A tall, slender man was seated behind the huge desk, his back to the door, gazing sightlessly out the window into the dark. He turned slowly, and I gasped. It was James.

"What are you doing here," he barked, his face harsh, his eyes glaring.

"James!" I exclaimed. How was it possible? I had just seen him walk out of the room and down the hall.

"Who did you think I was?" he inquired coolly.

"And Michael . . . who is . . . ?"

"Michael? He just left." A steely glint came into his eyes.

"I'm sorry. I don't understand . . ." I mumbled in confusion.

"You thought I was Michael. I see. Well, you might as well come in. It's time you knew. Please, sit down," he invited. He indicated a chair in front of the large desk. "First of all, Mrs. Fawkes, I should tell you that Michael and I are twins. Hence your confusion."

My mind reeled. Suddenly a number of things became clearer. The man in Skip's room that afternoon had been Michael, the doctor, not James deVergoff.

"Which one of you is the kidnapper—you or Michael?" I asked. "Or both?" I added grimly.

"Is that what you think I am—a kidnapper?" he asked.

"So it *was* you," I accused. It made sense. The tight lips, the cruel glint in his eyes, the emotionless stare—these were the features of the man who had kidnapped me. Not the gentle, caring features of the man I had met this afternoon.

"I was the man, yes. But I plead not guilty."

"Not guilty! What's your interpretation of a kidnapping!" I cried. "How would you like to be drugged and thrown into a plane like a bag of mail and carried miles from your home? Well, that's what you've done to me! Who do you think you are? Do you really suppose you're so far above the law?"

"In my opinion," he replied quite calmly, "it was simply an act of justice."

My mouth dropped open. "Justice! Are you serious?"

We sat staring at each other in silence for a moment.

"But what I want to know is *why* you did it. Was it because I was planning to run away? My decision to leave home had nothing to do with anyone but myself! I don't understand how you come into it at all. You seem to be rich...powerful. Could you have done this for money? It's a serious crime, you know! Martin may be my husband, but that doesn't entitle him to dispose of me in such a manner."

He looked at me for a moment and then spoke in a dry tone. "Your husband has nothing to do with this."

I nearly fell out of my chair.

"He had nothing at all to do with what you seem to insist on calling your 'kidnapping,'" he added.

I stared at him in disbelief. His face appeared to be carved from granite.

"However, that doesn't mean that he isn't responsible for it...in a way," he went on.

I frowned. What he was saying didn't make any sense. The doubt and confusion I was feeling must have been quite evident in my expression.

"I can well understand your lack of comprehension. I want you to listen to me now, without interruption. You have a right to know what's been going on and I'm quite willing to tell you."

"Finally," I sighed, nodding my head. I looked away from his tense face and my eyes fell on the glossy photograph of the young woman and child next to a slender vase holding a single rose. I didn't know why, but suddenly I sensed that his wife had something to do with all this.

James deVergoff lifted his hand to rub his forehead and I could see the wedding band on his ring finger. "It's a long story," he began in a low voice. Then he went on in a neutral tone, as though he wanted to keep all emotion out of what he was going to say. "It all started two years ago," he went on, "in Europe. In Brittany, actually. It was August."

He stopped and looked at me intently for a second before continuing. "It was a car accident. Does that tell you anything?"

"A car accident?" I repeated, confused. I tried to think back. "No, I don't think so. Should it?"

He didn't answer right away, but continued to stare at me pensively. Suddenly I felt quite ill at ease. His way of looking at me was making me very uncomfortable. There seemed to be such anger in his eyes. But what could I have done to cause that kind of anger in a man I didn't even know?

Then he rubbed his eyes with his hand, as though to chase away an unhappy sight. "It isn't important," he said flatly. "Only the facts are important." His voice was becoming more and more impersonal; it was obvious he was making a great effort to keep his feelings hidden.

"Two years ago, on August 27th, my wife and son were vacationing in France. They were in a car driven by my chauffeur. Another car ran into them, ramming them into a tree. My wife, Catherine, was killed. She was only twenty-six."

I opened my mouth to speak a few words of sympathy, but he stopped me before I could make a sound. "Please," he said. "No interruptions...remember?"

His face was hard, as though he was going over the tragedy in his mind. "My son was critically injured in the accident, but he managed to survive. He will never be able to walk again. He was four years old when it happened; now he's six. By some miracle my chauffeur escaped injury. He was able to tell me that the man driving the other car was drunk."

The heat in the room was becoming unbearable. My hands were perspiring. With the passing of every moment, I was becoming more uneasy.

"The driver took off without even stopping to see if he could help," he continued. "It wasn't until other cars came along that the police were called. By the time the ambulance arrived, my wife was in a coma. She died before they got her to the hospital. My son was saved. At least his life was saved, such as it is."

"And the other driver?" I heard myself asking.

"His car must have been damaged in the accident, because he had to stop at a garage down the road. The mechanic at the garage knew right away what had happened and forced him to return to the scene of the accident. He arrived at the same time as the ambulance. Somehow, it saved him from being charged with leaving the scene of the accident. I guess you could say he was lucky...depending on your point of view."

His voice had become quite bitter. I didn't say a word. I was too busy trying to cope with the incredible feeing of horror that was rising in me.

James deVergoff looked at me once more, his face a mask of reproach, and I could see that I was being accused. I shook my head violently and buried my face in my hands. I was trembling and could feel my cheeks burning.

Pitiless, he continued. "Do I have to tell you the name of that assassin? Aren't you already aware of this incident?"

I shook my head again. "I swear to you I know nothing about it."

"But you do know who I'm speaking of, don't you?" he demanded harshly.

What could I say? "Since you seem to believe that I'm involved in this somehow, then it must be someone close to me."

There was a long silence. He stared at me, his hand toying with a letter opener on the desk. A petal fell from the rose in front of the photograph of the beautiful young woman who had been his wife. Now she was dead because of someone's irresponsible behavior. She was smiling in the picture, quite lovely in her youthful happiness.

"It was Martin, wasn't it?" I said at last, tears choking my throat.

"Yes, Mrs. Fawkes, your husband was responsible for that dreadful accident."

"What can I say?" I stammered. "I'm sorry? Of course I'm sorry! It's horrible!"

I looked at him imploringly. "But are you absolutely sure he was drunk? Can you be sure that he left the scene of the accident? There must have been a police investigation, some kind of test. I've never heard anything about it."

I didn't even know why I was working so hard to find plausible arguments in defense of my husband. "Couldn't his car simply have gone out of control? Couldn't there have been some kind of mechanical failure? Martin has always been an excellent driver, but I have to admit that he likes to drive much too fast." Without realizing it, I was thinking out loud.

James deVergoff's harsh voice cut through the air like a sharp knife. "Precisely," he interrupted. "And the reason you heard nothing about it was that he paid everyone to keep quiet. He used his influence to bury the scandal. It wasn't the sort of thing that would exactly enhance his reputation. I couldn't understand how there could be a fatal accident without some kind of publicity. I laid charges, of course, but they were disregarded. Oh, a judgment was brought down, but since it was concluded that the accident was the result of some kind of mechanical failure over which the driver had no control, the charges were dismissed. There was no mention of the driver having left the scene of the accident, no question of his driving having been impaired. So I launched my own investigation. I went to France and hired two private detectives. Witnesses were found, including the owner of the garage and several motorists who had been on the same road at the time of the accident. The evidence I unearthed was quite conclusive, but the process had taken too much time. By then it was too late to appeal the original verdict."

He struck the top of the desk with his fist. "I can't let this man get away with it, no matter who his friends might be or how much money he has! That's why you are here, Mrs. Fawkes. I felt that you should know at least this much."

I looked at him, not really knowing what to say. To have been made aware of such a dreadful incident that way had been something of a shock. "But, I can't be held responsible," I murmured.

He lifted a hand in a conciliatory gesture. "That's true," he agreed. "But there's an old saying, madam: 'You can't make an omelet without breaking eggs.' I'm not suggesting that the action I have taken has been correct, or even proper, as far as you're concerned. I guess you could be called an innocent victim. Neither the first nor the last, I'd venture to say, in the matter of settling an account."

"I disagree," I protested violently. "Why should I have to suffer because of something my husband has done? Oh, I'd be the first to admit that Martin has his faults—many of them very serious. But that isn't any reason to kidnap me! You had no right to do such a thing."

His face was twisted, his eyes blazed madly. Anger and resentment were written all over his expression. He glared at me, clenching his teeth in an effort to control the trembling of his voice. "I loved my wife! Do you understand? Loved her without reservation, with a wild, savage love as untamed as I am. She was the focus of my life, the very heart of the only real happiness I have ever known. We had a son that was our pride and joy! Your husband destroyed my world. I was left with nothing but despair. He must be made to pay for it, Mrs. Fawkes. He must pay!"

James deVergoff got up and walked to the window. I could see only the back of him, his tall figure silhouetted against the light from the window. Perhaps he was turning away to hide the pain that was showing in his face. I felt very sorry for him.

Then he quickly turned around. "Now do you understand why you've been taken hostage?"

"Hostage?" I repeated. "Are you saying that you've asked for a ransom?"

With a sweep of his arm he cast away my suggestion as ridiculous. "Ransom? You mean money? Don't you know who I am?"

He spoke with arrogant disdain. It was quite obvious that I had offended him. He shrugged. "Money! You haven't understood a word I've been saying. I'm simply settling an account by taking payment in kind. He took my wife. So I'm taking his."

His simplistic, decisive way of interpreting the facts of my present situation terrified me. He believed that what he had done was just—in spite of the fact that it was insane. Surely he didn't expect me to agree to being his instrument of revenge. What was he going to do with me?

I began to wonder if perhaps the man's mind might have been affected by what had happened. And it struck me as ironic that I should be the one he had chosen. I would scarcely be missed. Now, if he had kidnapped Sylvia Gaylord he might have seen a very different reaction from Martin....

And yet, I had to wonder.... There could be no comparison between the love this man had felt for his wife and the shallow pretense practiced by Martin Fawkes, a man quite unable to have deep feelings for anyone.

All was quiet. James deVergoff appeared to be lost in thought. "You're not saying anything," he said finally.

I shrugged wearily. "I don't even know what my position is supposed to be in all of this. Besides, there isn't anything I could say that would change the situation. You brought me here by force, in spite of the fact that I had nothing to do with it!"

It was evident that he was making an effort to keep

himself under control. "I have nothing against you personally, Mrs. Fawkes. As I tried to explain earlier, you're simply a means to an end."

"Yes, I know...a pawn. It seems it never occurred to you that I might have feelings and thoughts of my own. You say that you have nothing against me personally. And yet you attacked me...personally. You had no right to do that!"

Once again his eyes blazed as he glared at me. "All right," he muttered. "So I had no right to do it! You tell me you were attacked? Well, think about it, Mrs. Fawkes. So was I! I'm simply making very sure that justice is finally done."

"By attacking the weak?" I interjected.

I could see the color rising in his face and knew immediately that I had struck him where it hurt. He stepped toward me and I wondered if he was going to hit me. It was obvious that he didn't like to be contradicted.

He stopped and stood staring at me, his eyes blazing with fury. I wondered if he could see fear in mine. Finally he looked away.

"It's true," he said in a quiet voice. "I did kidnap you. But do you really think I wanted to do so? It was merely part of my master plan."

I had to smile. "And do you really think that by kidnapping me you're going to deprive Martin of anything?"

"Of course," he replied with assurance. "And believe me, this is only the beginning."

He went on to explain as though he were outlining the intricacies of a problem in mathematics. "Your husband managed to avoid any consequences by covering up evidence that might point to him as a...murderer. In other words, he was completely cleared. His name didn't even appear in the newspapers. In fact, there was no mention of it anywhere, just as though nothing had happened. Well, I intend to see that the whole world is made aware of his crime. That's why I've laid such elaborate plans."

He started to pace once more, back and forth, back and forth, between the window and the door. "Oh, I know car accidents happen all the time. People are injured, even killed, nearly every day all over the world. Such things are treated as little more than trivia in the newspapers, usually a few lines buried in the back pages, and nobody pays any attention to them. Nobody, that is, except the insurance companies that have to pay the material losses. But my wife was everything to me and my son the greatest joy in my life. A brutal man took it all away from me in one drunken moment. And because he was powerful enough, he got away with it and went on about his business as though nothing had happened. Martin Fawkes doesn't seem to know what it means to have a conscience. The fact that a woman was killed and a small child crippled for life meant nothing at all to him.

"Do you wonder that I decided to take justice into my own hands? To me, this case has never been closed! It can't be reopened officially, of course, since judgment has been passed. But there are any number of ways to get publicity going. The kidnapping of Mrs. Fawkes should stir things up a little! It might just shake Martin Fawkes out of his placid existence. It's been driving me out of my mind, just thinking about that miserable man sleeping peacefully night after night without so much as a sign of remorse!"

I listened to him in some bewilderment, as he went on to describe his plan.

"I deliberately chose a time to accomplish this kidnapping when the media would be involved. Your husband has received a note explaining what has happened. No doubt he is doing everything he can to try to find you. I am sure he has already called the police. That's exactly what I want him to do."

So... Martin did know that I had been kidnapped. I was paralyzed. Would he leave me in the hands of the kidnappers, indifferent to my fate? I wasn't sure. I thought of telling James deVergoff about my last note to Martin and my leaving him, but I resisted. How would he respond to such news? Would he strike out at me in fury?

James deVergofff smiled sadly, a twisted, cruel smile. "The police will be at a loss at first, but it won't take them long to discover the traces I left behind so that they could find me. When they do, I'll explain the whole thing to them. Finally I'll have a way to bring out the truth about your husband's guilt and the things he did to escape justice. We'll stand face to face and I'll tear off the mask of innocence he's been wearing so successfully!"

"But why didn't you just go to him and settle it?" I protested.

"Because he was able to cover up the facts so well that I had no proof. Your husband, Mrs. Fawkes, is a man absolutely without conscience. Such a confrontation would have left him quite indifferent, perhaps even caustic. The only way to get to him is through some kind of scandal; it's the only thing he fears. He's terrified of losing face among his friends and clients."

He nodded his head and pressed his strong hands together. "These days, things can't be settled man to man. We no longer live in a time when an account can be settled by a duel. This is the so-called civilized age, and devious means must be employed to achieve one's ends. One must be cunning, and that's exactly what I've been!"

He lowered his head to look at his hands. "If you feel that you've been treated badly, I'm sorry. You aren't the one I'm trying to get at. But you were there, in the line of fire, and I had to use you."

Something about the way he said his last few words led me to think that our conversation was over. I got up. "I guess I'll just have to resign myself to it," I said in a cool voice. "But do you suppose I might ask a question?"

"Of course."

"Aren't you afraid that I might run away?"

His smile became sarcastic. "Running wouldn't do you much good here—you'd have to swim. And you won't find anyone willing to help you escape. My people are very loyal. No, I'm not worried about you running off. There's no possible way for you to leave the island."

I walked to the door, trying to appear as casual as possible. I needed time to think. He didn't know that I hadn't told him everything. I didn't want to mention that I had every intention of having him arrested and brought to trial once I was free. Nor did he know that Martin might not be looking for me—that he might, in fact, be welcoming the chance to torture me, in however deadly a manner. James deVergoff had prepared his ammunition very carefully and then fired his biggest guns. But I knew he had missed the target. He was living with false expectations.

What insane passion would be unleashed were he to learn that all he had worked for was in vain?

Chapter 10

The following day I spent with Skip. Now that I knew the mystery of why I was on the island, and also that there was no way for me to escape, I decided to spend as much of my time as I could helping the child. I took him outside into the sun. He was pale from continually remaining indoors, and after happy hours spent beside the pool, I was gratified to see a healthy pink blush on his cheeks.

True to his word, the young boy was making an incredible effort with his rehabilitation exercises. His nurse was amazed at his progress. My only enemy was Mauricia, who didn't try to hide her annoyance with the tedious and strenuous exercises the child was required to do. Indeed there were times when the pain brought tears to his eyes. But in spite of her gruff manner, I realized that Mauricia loved the little boy and suffered as much as he did, if not more.

How much longer would I be staying? In many ways I

didn't want to leave. Life was so pleasant, so heavenly there. I had no way of knowing how much time I had left. From what James deVergoff had said, I gathered that he was willing to wait for as long as it was necessary to get the attention he was after. I knew that it would take a while—and secretly I was glad.

While Skip and I played and worked on his exercises, I thought about what I had learned the night before. In so many ways I felt a tremendous sense of relief now that the questions had been answered. The craziness of the scheme still puzzled me, and I wondered what Michael's involvement was exactly, but these were minor questions compared to what I'd been struggling with before.

I could understand very well how Catherine deVergoff had been so happy here, living with a husband she adored and a child she cherished. Martin had a great deal to answer for. Even though the tragedy had been an accident, his carelessness had been the cause of it. He had destroyed the happiness of a young and loving couple and brought despair to a household that had once been filled with joy. Small wonder that James deVergoff had such a burning desire for revenge.

Having heard the dreadful verdict, I felt a very real hatred for my husband growing in me. A young boy's paralysis, a man's despair, a beautiful, happy woman's death...all his fault! And he never gave it a thought. He simply went on living his extravagant life—throwing parties, parading his mistresses for all the world to see, throwing away his money—without a care for the disaster he had brought to others.

I began to understand James deVergoff and had to agree with his bitter attitude. He had every reason to hate. And I was beginning to see a certain logic in his elaborately laid plans that would bring the vengeance he was seeking. What I couldn't understand was his willingness to throw everything away to get revenge. What would happen to Skip if James were sent to prison? The thought that James was insane crossed my mind once again.

WHEN I RETURNED to my room at five o'clock, I found recent editions of my husband's newspaper accompanied by a note that intrigued me. It was an invitation to have dinner with James deVergoff. To say the least, I was a little confused. He hadn't seemed to enjoy my company last night. Obviously he had changed his mind, and somehow the whole thing made me angry.

Who did this man think he was? Who did he think I was? Did he see me as some kind of puppet, whose strings could be pulled this way or that depending upon his most recent whim? Only yesterday he had insulted me, spoken to me without any regard for my feelings. Today he was asking if I would pay him the honor of having dinner with him.

My first reaction was to refuse. Then I realized that I would only be acting out of childish spite. Actually, I wanted to know more about my environment, having been dropped into it under such extraordinary circumstances. And I wanted to know more about the deVergoffs.

To quiet any fears I might have had, I told myself that he'd been offensive toward me before simply because he was under a great deal of tension when telling me about his wife's death. His hostility had increased at every mention of my husband's name. And he had only to see me to be reminded of his hatred for Martin. But, being a civilized man, he had reconsidered. Was I going to hold against him everything that had happened before? Was I going to gain anything by playing the role of the offended woman?

I had been brought here, after all, against my will. The fact that I was actually beginning to enjoy my stay was quite another matter. I still remained under the iron fist of my abductor, and it would be dangerous to contradict his orders. I would do much better by being diplomatic.

I turned my attention to the newspapers. Would there be any mention of the fact that the publisher's wife had been kidnapped? I almost knew what to expect: nothing. With pain in my heart, I searched the pages of the newsprint. Nowhere was there any mention of my disappearance or James deVergoff's letter to Martin. With a sinking heart I realized that my worst suspicions about my husband were true—that he was a heartless man. Worse than that, he was now, in my eyes, a murderer. He had no way of knowing that I was safe. For all he knew, my kidnappers could be torturing me. Yet his silence showed only one thing: his murderous indifference. I was stunned.

I thought of the invitation to dinner. Should I tell my kidnapper the reason for my husband's silence? What would he do to me then? Would he, in his frustrated rage, strike out at me? I didn't know. This was my only trump card, and it was to my advantage to hold on to it until I really needed it. At the least, I wanted time to consider the consequences. James was so vehement, so fanatical.

To ease my mind and heart, I turned to more practical considerations. I was faced with the problem of what to wear. The invitation had been couched in very formal terms. The wardrobe Christine had provided was quite charming and certainly adequate for the tropical climate on the island, but suitable only for daytime wear.

The only evening gown I had was the floor-length dress I

was wearing the evening I was kidnapped. It was what I would wear. I had no other choice.

I bathed and tended to my hair and dressed with the utmost care. When I went downstairs, I wanted to look my best. I added a touch of lipstick to my lips and green shadow to my eyelids. I needed very little makeup, actually. Even though I had only been on the island a few days, I had acquired a glowing tan. It suited me quite well.

A servant was waiting for me in the hallway. He was smiling broadly and his eyes expressed great pleasure. "Follow me, madam," he murmured. "The master has asked me to show you to the dining room. My name is Henry. I'm Mauricia's husband."

"Well, I'm glad to meet you, Henry!" I replied.

He led me to a vast, brightly lighted room in which a sumptuous table had been set. Silver candelabra graced the table and the place settings were of fine English bone china. The table had been set for three.

I didn't have much time to wonder who the third guest would be, for my eye caught a movement in front of the glass doors and I looked up to see my host. He was wearing a white dinner jacket and I was immediately reminded of the man in the tent the night of the reception...the night of my kidnapping. These thoughts raced through my mind as he came toward me across the dining room.

He stopped within a few steps of me and bowed gallantly. "Good evening, Mrs. Fawkes."

His tone seemed very grave. Puzzled, I looked at him, trying to define precisely what I was feeling. Slim and elegant in his dinner clothes, he was certainly very attractive.

"Good evening," I murmured with a small smile.

I was trying to find the right words to thank him for inviting me to dinner when he spoke up. "I hope I didn't frighten you last night."

His light tone seemed out of place. He was smiling, and the smile gave him a youthful air I had never seen before.

"Not really," I mumbled, trying to overcome my confusion. "But I got the impression that you didn't want to see me again...."

"You did? I...."

He was interrupted by the opening of the side door. I turned to see who was entering.

I put my hand to my mouth to muffle an exclamation of surprise. A second tall figure had appeared in the room, wearing a white dinner jacket and looking exactly like James deVergoff. It must be Michael, I thought to myself.

"Good evening, madam," said Michael. "Thank you for joining us." He walked to me and extended his hand. Reluctantly, I lifted my hand. It was a very proper handshake.

I dropped my hand to my side and looked back and forth from one to the other. I shook my head. Two tall, slender figures. Two white dinner jackets. They were so alike they could have been carbon copies of each other.

"You seem confused, madam. Is it because of me?" one asked.

"I'm so sorry," interrupted the other man. "I forgot to introduce you to my brother. Michael, this is Vivian Fawkes."

Michael looked at me piercingly. "Yes," he said softly. "We've met."

I blushed, in spite of myself. Baffled, I continued to look from one to the other, quite unable to speak. I had never seen them together, and the effect was unnerving. The only way I could tell the two apart was by the occasional, subtle twitching in James's eyes, and a cold, hard look he often had. Michael's face, although the features were nearly identical to his brother's, appeared friendly and relaxed.

I took a deep breath. I was beginning to understand. But I still couldn't help looking back and forth from one to the other. "The resemblance is quite remarkable," I murmured. "Extraordinary!"

Michael deVergoff seemed much more at ease, as though once the introductions were over the situation offered little out of the ordinary. "Everyone gets us mixed up," he said with a grin.

I noticed that their voices were distinctly different. Michael's was several tones deeper.

As we were exchanging these few words, James had gone to get some punch and was bringing the glasses back on a tray. "Now then," he said, "let's have a toast. To your stay here, Mrs. Fawkes. May it be as brief as possible. I'm sure that's what you're hoping."

"Of course," I said, mouthing a conviction I didn't feel.

There was a moment of embarrassed silence. James was frowning and his face looked quite sad. "Did you read the newspapers?" he asked finally.

"Yes. . . . And thanks, by the way. It was thoughtful of you to have them sent to my room."

"There's no mention of your, uh, absence."

"You mean my kidnapping," I shot back.

"Well, if that's what you want to call it," he conceded with a shrug.

"Come, come," Michael intervened. "We've invited Mrs. Fawkes to dinner to make things a little more pleasant for her. Let's not talk about anything unpleasant. She's our guest; we'll just forget the rest of it for the moment."

"I suppose you're right," agreed his brother with little enthusiasm.

Contrary to what I had originally believed, I was beginning to get the impression that the invitation to dinner had come from Michael. I wondered what he thought of the treatment to which I'd been subjected. Had he been aware of the kidnapping?

The operation had not been carried out without risk. The circumstances under which I had been brought to James deVergoff's house constituted intolerable abuse and I had every right to be more than angry. Kidnapping was one of the worst possible crimes in any country.

Suddenly, Henry appeared in the doorway. "Madam," he announced very formally, "dinner is served."

That the announcement had been made directly to me came as a pleasant surprise. It was a definite sign that my two hosts were capable of recognizing the proprieties, and I appreciated it. I also found it confusing. Their behavior alternated between brutality and sophistication so often that I decided to give up trying to figure it out.

We got through dinner without any of the embarrassment or constraint I had been fearing. I had to admit that my first meal with the deVergoff brothers was not only delicious, but also very pleasant.

The food was typically Caribbean in taste and presentation. Each of the dishes had been beautifully seasoned with the local spices. The main staple, it seemed, was fish, and it was served in succulent variety.

"I'm afraid you can't look forward to anything but Creole cooking here," warned Michael. "Our servants don't know a thing about any other type of cooking."

I protested that I had become very appreciative of the

different flavors peculiar to the food since I had arrived on the island.

"It's a curious mixture of French and Spanish cooking with a few twists that are unique to the Caribbean," continued my dinner companion. "Not to mention a small contribution from Africa."

It was quite evident that both men were making every effort to keep the conversation on neutral ground. With remarkable dexterity, Michael steered the talk from the mores of the inhabitants to the richness of the land and sea and then even explained the costumes of the native people.

From time to time his brother would make a remark, but I had the feeling that he wasn't really with us. His mind was elsewhere, absorbed, no doubt, in the cruel thoughts that appeared to obsess him.

However, there was one subject that did provoke James's interest. "Have you had a chance to explore the island?" he asked.

"A little bit," I replied, trying to appear offhand. What little exploring I had done had been motivated by a wish to escape. "I hope to do more soon," I continued. "I'm looking forward to it."

"You'll find there's lots to see," stated Michael. "The village, the sugarcane factory, the rum distillery...and of course, the people living here."

"Are there many people on the island?" I asked.

"Seventeen hundred, including those working in this household."

"The people here lead an easygoing life," declared James. "They work when they want to and stop when they want to. The island provides all the food they need. Fish and fruit and vegetables are plentiful and within easy reach. And, unlike most of the other islands of the archipelago, the houses here are very comfortable. They're real stone houses that were built at the time of this plantation's beginnings, around 1700."

"Let me add, intervened Michael, "that my brother does all he can to keep this place as rustic and romantic and, incidentally, authentic as possible. For instance, you won't find a television set anywhere on the island."

"That's right!" James shot back, his voice rising. "Can't you just see television antennae sticking up all over the place, ruining every bit of the natural beauty? Oh, I know—some people call that progress. Well, I don't happen to agree! I've fought like mad against the so-called advance of civilization on this island. It's our home; we've owned it for centuries! And I simply won't stand by and see it opened up to the kind of commercial enterprise that would bring everything here from packaged vitamins to credit cards. I don't want our people to have those things; I don't think they need them!"

"Well, you can't hold back progress forever," murmured Michael, his tone a little dubious. "Being so isolated has allowed us to live in relative peace and quiet until now, apart from the unrest that seems to have pervaded most of the rest of the world. But people are visiting the other islands, remember. When they see the automatic washers and dryers, the cars, the television sets—"

"They'll be glad to get home where they can live quite comfortably without any of those things. We're fortunate to be living in peaceful isolation and I intend to do everything I can to maintain the sanity and stability that life on this island affords our people. We're not entirely primitive, after all. Every single house has indoor plumbing."

"Imagine," murmured Michael wryly. "Indoor plumb-

ing.... And we even have air conditioning here in the
main house...in one of the engineers' houses, too! Let's
face it, James—progress is definitely making inroads, like
it or not. And one of these days, I'm afraid everything will
likely change."

"And with the change will come the end of our happy,
peaceful life," declared James. "That's what I'm trying to
prevent for as long as I can. Not just for myself, but for the
rest of the people who live here, too."

"I'm afraid it's the old dream of Utopia," sighed Michael.
"Mind you, I have to agree with you. I'm just not the op-
timist you are, that's all."

"Well, I'll know I fought to the very end," stated James,
his eyes veiled, his mouth a thin, taut line. "At least I'll
have that much."

He used the same resolute tone I had noticed the evening
before. I realized that this was something of a personal
conversation between the two brothers. Michael's ideas
seemed to be a little more modern than James's, but I had
to concede that James had every right to his opinions. Why
shouldn't he try everything possible to keep his paradise
intact?

As soon as we had finished our meal, James announced
that he was leaving us in order to go to his son. I took advantage of the situation to turn the conversation to a subject that really interested me. I told my host that I enjoyed
spending time with Skip every day, playing and talking
with him. For the first time, I thought I could see a degree
of warmth in his eyes as he looked at me thoughtfully.

"You're interested in my son?" he asked.

"He's very lovable," I said. "I like him very much and he
seems to enjoy my company."

"Well, he certainly should be getting more attention

than he does," he said sadly. "He's the victim of such gross injustice!"

There was a moment of silence. His face twisted, as it did every time the suggestion of his obsession came up. Then he turned his attention to me once more.

"I think it's good for Harold if you spend some time with him. However, I understand that you're making my son cry. Evidently those exercises you're putting him through can be quite painful." His expression had turned suddenly from one of pleasure to displeasure, and I was completely taken aback.

"He forgets all about the pain when he sees how well he's getting along," I replied.

"I simply will not tolerate it!" he declared.

"Would you rather have him remain the way he is?" I asked. "Don't you want him to make as much progress as he possibly can?"

"I don't think you're qualified to judge just how much progress he might be expected to make," he said in a cold voice. "After all, you're not a doctor."

I noticed that Michael was intentionally quiet, and I suspected that this was a frequent argument between them.

"That's true," I agreed. "But it just so happens that I'm a doctor's daughter. I also studied to become a physical therapist. Furthermore, when I was a little girl, my brother had a condition that was very much like your son's. Faith and determination succeeded where medical treatment failed. He succeeded to a point . . . at least to the extent that he was able to make something of his life."

"Are you saying that there actually was a significant recovery?" His voice registered disbelief.

"Well, no two cases are alike, of course. But in this instance there was progress to some degree. Indeed, there was enough progress to permit a somewhat normal life. Don't you think it's worth a try?"

I had spoken with a certain vehemence and Michael, who had kept out of the conversation to that point, spoke up in support of my theory. "What Mrs. Fawkes is saying is right, James," he said quietly, "as I have argued many a time."

"Consultations with some of the most renowned doctors in the world left me no hope," retorted James with a shrug.

"But there's always an unknown factor! And since Skip seems quite willing to do the exercises—"

"But he's suffering! He's only torturing himself, playing this cruel game. I simply will not allow him to be unhappy."

"Oh, there's a certain amount of physical pain, James," Michael continued. "We have to expect that. But there's something else that might be seen to be much more important. Skip can live with the pain because there's the possibility that by putting up with it, he's helping himself to get better. In other words, for the first time since the accident, he has hope!" Michael paused and looked at his brother. "No matter what his discomfort may be, that glimmer of hope has to make him happy!"

"But what if he fails to improve? His hopes will have risen, and all the work he has done will come to nothing. It would break his heart."

I thought that Michael had passed a reasonable judgment and realized that he was much more able to be objective than his brother when there was question of anything concerning the boy. Skip, after all, was James's son. He couldn't see that if Skip never tried, he would never get better.

"Please," I implored. "Let me try, at least. In the very

short time I've had with Skip, he's already shown some improvement. And he doesn't even cry anymore. He's very cheerful about the exercises."

"Well, okay," James muttered begrudgingly.

"Time is the one thing of which I seem to have a plentiful supply," I assured him. "Believe me, it'll be good for both of us."

He frowned. My ambiguous reply didn't seem to please him, since he could read the innuendo in it. "It won't be for long," he mumbled. "But I thank you anyway."

He went out of the room, leaving me alone with his brother. I was uncomfortably aware that Michael and I were now alone, and of his closeness to me. I shifted nervously in my chair and fiddled with a spoon, not knowing what to say.

"Why don't we have our coffee outside," Michael suggested, his deep, gentle voice reassuring me and putting me at ease.

"An excellent idea." I smiled at him. The heat of the day had dissipated and it was quite refreshing outdoors.

Henry served us at the pool side. The floodlights in the pool area were reflected among the tall trees, making it seem like a fairyland. The air was wonderfully soft and the warm breeze caressed my skin.

My companion was silent. There was still an embarrassment between us—due in part, no doubt, to the incredible situation in which I had found myself. I would have given a lot to know what Michael was thinking and whether or not he agreed with his brother. But he wasn't saying anything.

While Henry poured the coffee, Michael got up and walked to the veranda. He came back carrying a small transistor radio, which he turned on. A song floated on the air. Gradually my uneasiness disappeared. I thought about the two men living here alone in the vast house filled with servants, memories, ghosts from the past.

Suddenly the sound of Michael's voice startled me. He was posing a question that seemed incongruous. "Do you like children?" he asked.

I was confused for a moment and then remembered my discussion with James before he had left. "Yes," I replied warmly. "As a matter of fact, I do." I stopped for a moment and then added with a note of melancholy, "Unfortunately, I've never had any."

"I know," he said simply.

I turned to look at him. He seemed to understand my surprise and silent question. "If you had children," he answered before I had a chance to ask, "my brother would never have kidnapped you."

"So, you do know about it!" I burst out, but I was interrupted by Henry, who informed Michael that there was a medical emergency in the village.

"I'm sorry. I must run," Michael said, jumping to his feet.

"I understand," I started to say, but before I could even finish he was gone.

I laughed. It was a scene all too familiar from my childhood. So many times, my father had had to jump up from family gatherings to attend to some crisis.

I lingered over my coffee in silence, enjoying the sounds of the evening, and the lights playing on the surface of the water. So Michael did know that I'd been kidnapped. I remembered overhearing him say, "How could you do it?" to James the night before. Was he referring to the kidnapping? Or was he an accomplice to the crime, and talking about something else entirely?

Guilty or not, I had to admit that I'd enjoyed Michael's company that evening, despite the tension that James carried with him, and the arguments he provoked. In spite of myself, I looked forward to the days ahead.

Chapter 11

The next morning I was surprised by Michael bringing my breakfast tray to my door.

"Good morning," he said with an endearing grin. "I'm sorry that I was called away so abruptly last night. I was looking forward to spending the evening with you. Forgive me?"

"Of course!" I responded, somewhat embarrassed at having been caught by him on awaking.

"Well...here's your breakfast. I ambushed Lucille in the hallway for it. I wondered if you might enjoy going out for a cruise today."

"I'd love to, but...." I hesitated. After what had happened two days before in Skip's room, I didn't know if I could trust him, much less myself.

"I know what you're thinking. I've been wanting to tell you that I'm sorry. I got carried away. I know it sounds like a poor excuse, but I couldn't help myself. I promise you, it will never happen again."

"Please...don't apologize," I begged. "I understand. And of course I'll go. I'd love to."

"Good. How would you like to meet me at the front door in a couple of hours, then...say ten o'clock?"

I nodded in agreement.

"Bring your bathing suit. We can go for a swim if you like," he added before setting the tray down and leaving.

I was delighted, although still somewhat nervous about being alone with him after what had happened.

Christine prepared a picnic basket for us and we both left the house happily, heading for the cove where his boat was docked. To reach it we had to cross the southernmost tip of the island. The day was sunny and beautiful and I couldn't help looking at the scenery around me with more than a little awe. Michael was driving a Land Rover, which, together with James's jeep and the old truck, completed the deVergoff fleet of vehicles.

"You're a curious woman," stated Michael suddenly, a half smile on his lips. He seemed relaxed, leaning comfortably back, steering the Land Rover easily with one hand.

"I am?" I replied in surprise.

"The way you've been acting, one would think you had chosen this place to spend your vacation. You don't seem to be holding any grudge for having been treated the way you've been."

He smiled in my direction and my heart soared. Today he seemed more handsome, more strong and sensual than ever.

"Well, that's something that will have to wait until later on to be settled," I replied a little pompously, teasing him.

"Yes, I would expect that you intend to lay charges," he responded seriously. "But in spite of that, you've been charming. You appear to be very happy and certainly have shown us—and especially Skip—a great deal of kindness."

"Good heavens! You're making me sound like a paragon of virtue!" I laughed. I couldn't help feeling a little embarrassed at the extravagance of his compliments.

"Not at all," he said. "Besides all that, you don't seem to be even slightly sad at having left behind everything and everyone you know."

I made an effort to appear casual. "Oh, I'm quite sure that this crazy kidnapping isn't going to lead to anything. Besides, my exile here won't last forever."

He frowned slightly and his face showed confusion. "Just the same, for the victim of a kidnapping, I have to say that you certainly haven't been much of a problem to your kidnappers."

"Don't count on it," I replied, still in a light tone. "Appearances can be very deceiving, you know."

"True," he murmured. "But no matter what you might be trying to tell me, you've been behaving like a friend of the family, or even a relative."

"Do many of your relatives come here to visit?" I asked, hoping to change the subject.

"Since Catherine died, we haven't invited anyone here," he said soberly after a moment of hesitation.

He seemed ready to confide in me, but unfortunately, we arrived at that moment at the cove where his yacht was docked. Michael parked his car close to a fisherman's house that also served as an inn for the island. There were tables set up outside under the coconut trees. A native woman came out of the house, greeted Michael and offered us some refreshments.

"This is Anna," explained Michael cordially. "She's an absolutely divine cook!"

"May I fix you something for lunch?" she asked with a broad smile.

"No, thank you, Anna. We've brought a picnic basket with us and will eat on the outer island," Michael replied.

He gestured with his hand toward a small green spot out in the ocean that was scarecely visible from where we were situated. "That's the island where I spent most of my childhood," he explained. "We used to fish there and let our fish dry in the sun. Now the island is abandoned."

We boarded the yacht and Michael skillfully maneuvered it out of the bay. In a very short while I could make out the shores of the tiny island with its lush vegetation. The palm trees swayed in the warm breeze and the coconut trees hung their heavy heads over the water. It was a glorious sight.

Never before had I seen sand so fine and white. Michael moored the boat at the water's edge and we climbed a dune to see the old house on the other side. It was made of wood and had an air of once having been occupied. On the veranda and around the house there were weather-beaten wooden benches and there was a small shed that was half-destroyed.

I was intrigued by large holes in the sand and asked Michael what caused them.

"That's where the crabs hide," he explained. "It's a species that can't be found anywhere else but here. They're enormous!"

I was terrified of anything that crawled and when he took hold of one of the crabs by a leg to show it to me I let out a horrified scream.

"Don't be afraid. It won't bite!" he said with a laugh. "Just try not to step on one."

It was enough to cause the place to lose some of its

charm for me, but my companion happily chased away my doubts.

"Let's go for a swim," he suggested.

"Let's!" I agreed enthusiastically.

He showed me a place in the dense foliage where I could change into my bathing suit in complete privacy. Within a few minutes we were swimming in the emerald waters. The water was very clear and we could see the various fish swimming close by and the shells on the bottom. It was a beautiful place of peace and solitude.

Michael swam with graceful ease. It was obvious he was in his element. We stayed in the water for quite a long time and when I finally came out, I was filled with a great sense of well-being. I stretched out on the sand and waited for my companion to join me.

A shadow fell across the sparkling sand and I lifted my head to see Michael's smiling face.

He held out his hands. "Come on! A run on the beach will do us a world of good!"

He helped me to my feet and I ran across the moist sand at the edge of the water. He started after me and caught up with me very quickly, taking hold of my wrist. Delighted, I was quite breathless.

In this wild, unspoiled setting we were like a couple of children. I hadn't known a joy so beautiful, so simple, in a very long time. Even as a child I had never felt so young. And Michael seemed to be feeling the same way. He radiated strength and good health.

I stepped a little behind him, playfully tugging and trying to escape him.

"You're my prisoner," he said happily.

His unfortunate choice of words broke the spell. With a

small frown, he suddenly let go of my wrist. "How about lunch?" he proposed, his tone deliberately neutral.

Then, turning quickly, he walked away from me toward the dune. I stood watching him for a few seconds and then followed, feeling the warmth under my feet as I moved across the sand.

Suddenly, a giant crab came up from his hole in the sand directly in front of me. In spite of myself, I screamed.

Michael wheeled around immediately. "What is it?" he called.

I stood pointing at the slow-moving creature. "I'm sorry," I said, trying to laugh. "I just can't help it—they really do frighten me."

"No need to apologize," he comforted me.

He came back and took me by the shoulder, his touch light and caring. Gently, he guided me to one of the benches close to the old house. I was aware only of his hand touching me, sending thrills through my sun-warmed body.

"The crabs won't be able to get at you here," he said in a teasing tone that made me laugh. "What the doctor orders to remedy a case of the screams is food." With that, he started to take the food out of the picnic basket. I shook my head at his good humor, and after a moment, I helped him lay out our lunch of fruit and pastries.

When we had finished eating, Michael led me to the veranda of the old house. Choosing the best of several battered chairs, he offered it to me and then sat down facing me. "It's too hot to move," he said with a sigh.

I leaned back in my chair luxuriously. My eyelids were drooping and I looked at him through half-closed eyes.

Had we not been sitting in the shade, the heat of the afternoon would have been unbearable. The only sounds to be heard were the waves breaking against the shoreline and the rustle of leaves as the slight breeze moved among the palm trees. I was quite relaxed. And I was very, very happy.

Michael, however, seemed unable to recapture his lighthearted mood. He was frowning as he smoked and appeared to be worried about something. "This kidnapping business is completely insane," he said suddenly, his tone exasperated.

I opened my eyes, reluctantly pulling myself out of my daydreaming into reality. "You're telling me?" I said with all the dignity I could muster.

He looked at me, his deep blue eyes penetrating. "I can't understand how you've managed to keep your wits about you," he finally said slowly.

"You call my outburst yesterday keeping my wits about me?" I laughed.

"It was entirely understandable under the circumstances. At the time I didn't know the truth. My brother had told me that you were the wife of a client of his in need of special psychiatric treatment—of what we call an R and R, rest and recuperation—following what I had been told was a rather rough stint in a mental hospital. I thought your crying about kidnapping was a psychotic fantasy. It wasn't until later that I realized how emotionally healthy you are. Most psychotics don't respond directly to a situation. They're lost in a world of their own. You, on the other hand, were never distant. . . ."

I cringed inwardly, thinking of how far from distant I had been, how uncontrollably he had aroused my passion. Uncomfortably, I turned from him and gazed out to sea. "I didn't know you were a psychiatrist," I said, trying to change the subject.

"I used to be. I'm not anymore, although I can certainly stand in as one in a pinch. Before I came here I was head of Kensington Hospital in Miami. . . ."

"I've heard of it. It's quite famous, isn't it?" I broke in quickly.

"Yes. I suppose it is. We conducted original research there that attracted a number of top surgeons from around the world. I loved my work, but when Catherine was killed, James completely went to pieces and needed my help. And, of course, Skip needed a great deal of both physical and emotional attention that his father was too weak and too upset to give. So I left my work and came here."

"That was kind of you. Not many brothers would take on that kind of responsibility," I replied, moved by the generosity he was displaying.

"Well. . .the situation was an unusual one. In fact, there's something I must tell you because it will help you understand what has been done to you. However, I urge you never to repeat it to anyone—not that I have the right to ask any favor of you, considering. . . ."

"It doesn't matter. . .I promise," I eagerly reassured him.

"My brother's breakdown was of a mental nature—as well as a physical one. The shock of his wife's death brought on a fairly severe heart attack. But he also lapsed into a form of psychosis that was very difficult to treat. Had I not been here to look after him, to treat him, as well as take care of all the business matters pertaining to the running of the estate, he would have been hospitalized. And after all the grief he'd already been through, I knew that would kill him. I had to stay. I had no other choice.

"Since then, however, I've come to love the land of my childhood once again. And I'm also finding that setting up hospitals and medical facilities in these out-of-the-way places where they're really needed is extremely rewarding—more so, in fact, than my prestigious work as the head of a world-renowned hospital.

"But that's enough of my history. Tell me about youself . . . your husband, your exciting life in the most important city in the world. What a change it must be from this quiet spot! You must be bored to tears."

I laughed and shifted uncomfortably in my chair. "Not in the least. I love it here," I confessed. "It's like you said—it's like being on a vacation, rather than in a prison."

"Well, I'm glad there have been some rewards. I know that much of this experience could only have been extremely terrifying to you."

"Yes, that's true, too," I confessed, biting my lip at the memory of that night. "Thank you for explaining about your brother. Do you think that what he has done is part of the same . . . mental problem?"

I was trying to appear tactful, but I found the revelation of James's insanity frightening.

"I can only conclude that it is," Michael replied. "If only I had recognized his condition and discovered his plans sooner. I'm afraid I'd lapsed into thinking he was much better. I was so pleased when he expressed a desire to become involved again in the running of the plantation by saying that he wanted to make trips to New York. Of course, I welcomed the idea. The plantation work was taking me away from what really interested me—the setting up of the hospitals. It didn't occur to me. . . .

"You see," he went on, "I must take responsibility. I should have known that this might happen. After your husband was acquitted, James went into a wild state. I found it almost impossible to control him. He wanted to hunt your husband down and shoot him, and might very well have done so. So when James came up with his plan to bring the whole thing to the attention of the public and, he hoped, eventually to some kind of justice, it seemed like a much better solution than roaring off into the night with a gun in his hand and fire in his eyes. He calmed down and started to work out the details with great care. Naturally, I was glad to see him apparently in control of himself. I never thought for a minute that he really meant to go ahead with it. I thought time would heal his pain and anger, and when he asked me to help him, I turned him down flat. I thought that was the end of it. I didn't know he had chosen to proceed in secret."

He looked at me. "Believe me," he said quietly, "I'm really sorry."

"But you knew my name. Didn't that ring any bells?" I asked.

"No. You see, I never knew the name of the man who killed Catherine.... Forgive me, Vivian, for referring to your husband in that way. I'm afraid that I, too, can only think of him as Catherine's murderer."

"I understand," I said, choking back tears. "Believe me, I do."

Michael looked at me with curiosity in his eyes. He took my hand in his, stroked it, then started suddenly and withdrew. Sheepishly, he looked skyward and grinned. "I know," he said. "I promised."

I ached to return his touch. Instead I gazed sternly at the horizon. As it was, my emotions were raging.

"There's something I must ask you," Michael ventured tentatively.

"Yes?" I answered tremulously.

"I don't understand why your husband hasn't responded to James's threats."

I sat in silence. That was the one thing I did not want to discuss.

"Tell me, Vivian...why hasn't he responded? Isn't he worried for your safety?" Michael insisted.

I considered lying, saying that I was sure my husband was concerned, worried sick with grief, and that no doubt he was working cleverly in secret with all the private detectives he could muster.

"I don't know," I said instead, the insecurity and hurt showing in my voice. "I'm as much in the dark as you are."

Again, he examined me with curiosity. I could sense that he wanted to press for more information, but he hesitated.

"How did James manage it?" I asked, changing the subject. "The kidnapping, I mean."

"It wasn't easy. Apparently my brother had had your husband thoroughly investigated and was familiar with his habits. And he had a detailed floor plan of your house. Your party was publicized well in advance in the newspapers so he decided to take advantage of the general confusion. It took a certain amount of preparation, of course, not to mention a lot of money. He arranged to have some of our people hired by your catering service and to have two reliable men with him."

"Good Lord! He certainly was organized!" I exclaimed.

"Yes," he agreed with a wry smile. "From what I've pieced together, the car was parked close to your front gate, and as the sightseers began to leave, he just kept moving it closer and closer. You know the rest...."

"Yes.... I can still hear that waiter telling me someone wanted to see me at the front gate. I made it easy for him, didn't I? Walked right into his little trap. Within ten seconds I was out like a light. It's like something out of a mystery! Well, you might as well tell me the rest. What happened then?" I inquired eagerly, shifting in the chair to a more comfortable position.

"He put you in the car and drove to our private plane. You must have been sleeping like a baby."

"You'd sleep like a baby, too, if somebody dosed you with chloroform!" I exclaimed with returning indignation.

"It wasn't chloroform," he protested. "James did a little research in my medical texts and made very sure that he used something that wouldn't hurt you in any way."

"Thought of everything, didn't he?" I muttered bitterly.

"To sum it all up," Michael continued without being asked, "you apparently suffered very little inconvenience throughout the whole flight. James said that you slept very quietly. And when I took you in my arms to carry you to the Land Rover when the plane landed—"

I jumped to my feet. "Took me in your arms!"

"Naturally! You were sound asleep! James had explained that you needed sedation for the trip because of your unstable emotional condition. And I believed him. You kept right on sleeping through the ride from the airstrip to the house. So I picked you up again and carried you into the house. It was like carrying a bouquet of flowers. When I put you down on the bed in your room, you looked just like Sleeping Beauty . . . in a green dress!"

Suddenly a thought occurred to me and I blushed. I remembered that the next morning, when I woke up, I was not wearing my own clothes.

"And who . . . who undressed me?" I asked tentatively.

"Don't worry," he said with a wry grin. "It wasn't me. Mind you, I would have been quite happy to do it, but

Christine was there and I thought it might be better if she were to take over. Right?"

I could feel my whole face burning. Now he was teasing me! His eyes were gently laughing and I had to laugh with him. Besides, it was difficult to be angry with anyone as charming as he was.

He seemed to make a sudden decision. "Listen," he said quite seriously. "This can't go on. I'll have to get you back to New York."

I sat up in my chair. "When?"

"As soon as possible. Tomorrow, maybe?"

"Tomorrow?" I echoed with a definite lack of enthusiasm.

Puzzled, he looked at me. "Aren't you glad?"

"But . . . your brother . . . ." I fumbled.

"My brother? Yes, that is the problem."

He sat deep in thought for a moment. "I think he must be asking himself a few questions, too," he said finally. "If you want the truth, I believe you're becoming something of an embarrassment to him."

It didn't surprise me. Somehow I seemed to have a talent for becoming an embarrassment. Martin wasn't doing a thing to find me and the deVergoff brothers couldn't wait to get rid of me.

"Do you really think he'll let me go?" I queried.

He shook his head doubtfully. "I just don't know. He can be very stubborn sometimes."

Michael looked away from me and I could see the tension in his body. "Thank God his hatred doesn't seem to be directed at you."

"Oh, he's always been quite proper with me. In fact, he almost seems to like me," I replied, trying to adopt a light tone.

"You've disarmed him," replied Michael. "You've been taking an interest in his son."

"My friendship with Skip was quite spontaneous and I happen to believe that it works both ways," I stated vehemently.

"Oh, I believe so, too. It certainly isn't much fun to be six years old and handicapped the way Skip is," Michael replied.

"I don't understand why his father hasn't been more interested in his rehabilitation. He must know that the boy can make a certain amount of progress."

"I can't answer that. I've advised him many times, but he just seems to cling to a negative viewpoint. Unfortunately, that affects Skip's outlook. And, as you know, the patient's attitude is vital for recovery," Michael concluded with a discouraged sigh.

I told him about my brother, Simon.

His eyes looking far out to sea, Michael sat in silence, listening without interruption. "Wouldn't it be marvelous if Skip could get better," he mused thoughtfully when I had finished. "Even if he could manage to move around a little, just enough so that he could have a decent life!"

As he spoke, his voice grew soft and warm and I could see the emotion in his face.

"You love your nephew very much, don't you?" I said quietly.

He didn't answer immediately. He seemed to be looking inward at images and scenes he thought he had forgotten.

"Yes," he said, almost in a whisper. "I love Skip. He's all I have left of his mother."

Before I could control it, my hand involuntarily flew to my mouth in a gesture of surprise. Of course, he saw the motion.

"Oh, there was nothing between us," he explained. "Catherine never knew how much I loved her."

Again, he looked out to sea. I waited.

"Maybe it had something to do with James and I being twins. I don't know.... They say that sometimes twins have the same feelings, the same emotions, simultaneously. James and I were together when we met Catherine and we both fell in love with her. She chose James. They were very happy together. Neither of them ever realized how disappointed I was. Somehow I managed to hide it. I moved to Miami and immersed myself in my career. Time went by, and of course I got over it. To a large extent, anyway."

He went on speaking for a long time, looking out to sea as though he were alone, talking to himself. I had never known a man could be as kind and generous as Michael was revealing himself to be. He was the antithesis of my husband.

Suddenly he got up from his chair and took a few steps. "I wonder why I'm telling you all this," he said. "I've never said a word to anyone else...."

He thought for a few seconds and I waited in silence, lacking the courage to express the sympathy I was feeling in my heart.

"It must be because you're a stranger," he added. "You've walked into my life out of nowhere and I fear that you'll walk out of it the same way."

He was quite right. I was a stranger. I was going away. There was nothing else for me to do. He had said it himself. This couldn't go on.

I got up from my chair and together we stepped off the veranda and walked to the top of the dune.

THAT EVENING, I did some thinking about what had taken place in the previous few hours. Certainly I had learned a great deal. For one thing, I was beginning to know the Michael deVergoff who had intrigued me so much.

The day had served to bring us quite close together. I felt that we had become friends in many ways. It had been a day of enchantment and I couldn't help thinking about it, particularly the return trip on Michael's yacht over water that was as smooth as glass.

As I leaned over the railing, I could see the bottom of the bay. The water was very clean and, reflecting the sky, appeared blue. Pink coral, like fine lace, sparkled on the bottom, threaded with a variety of multicolored shells. A seemingly endless variety of small exotic fish darted in and out of the fantastic formations. The whole thing seemed quite unreal.

Michael had turned off the motor and come to stand at the railing next to me. I looked toward the shore of St. Victor Island. It was all too close. I could see the houses and fields and a few natives. I turned to look at what seemed to be a cloud of vapor. It was the Tilsun volcano.

"There's been smoke coming out of it the last few days," remarked my companion.

I said nothing. I simply wanted to enjoy those few minutes, knowing that everything that was happening was all very precarious and any happiness I might be enjoying was nothing but fleeting.

Michael put his hand on my shoulder. I loved the feel of that hand against my skin.

I turned toward him and he took me in his arms, kissing me fully, insistently, pressing my body into his. His body was hungry, wanting, urgent, and I melted into an eternity of desire, where all that mattered were his lips, his hair, his arms, his hands. . . .

He held my face in his hands, kissing me tenderly, again

and again, murmuring my name. I closed my eyes, feeling the miracle of his breathing, only wanting to be with him, in his arms, forever and ever.

"I'm sorry, Vivian," he said huskily. "If you only knew how hard it's been not to . . . ."

He pulled away reluctantly. "Vivian, may I tell you something?" he asked seriously.

I nodded, unable to trust my voice to speak.

"I know I have no rights in the matter, that you are a happily married woman, but I must tell you anyway. I've cared for you ever since I carried you off that plane."

I turned away. I couldn't bear to hear the tenderness and warmth in his voice, see the love in his eyes. I would be leaving in a few days. There was nothing more to say. I felt stricken.

"Don't look so sad!" Michael laughed. "After all, I might have said that I hated you. Would that make you feel any better?"

I laughed, loving his ease, loving his humor.

"Had you been free, you know," he added with an impish grin, "I might very well have kidnapped you for myself."

I laughed. How could I tell this man that I thanked fate for having steered me into his arms at a time when my life had become unbearable? Of course, I couldn't allow myself to say any of those things. His brother had kidnapped me. I would be leaving soon, flying back to the reality of my life in New York. Those were the facts.

But when he picked me up in his arms to carry me to shore at the end of our day together, neither could I let him know that in my heart there was a joy I had never known before.

Vivian, I told myself sternly, *I think you're in for a very hard time.*

Chapter 12

The day after our excursion to the small island, Michael left on one of his business trips. It was harvest time for the sugarcane and the whole island was a hive of activity. James was working practically around the clock. When he did manage a few moments at the house during the next week, he seemed very weary.

I devoted almost all of my time that week to young Skip. I knew that my stay on St. Victor Island would be coming to an end very soon and I wanted to help Skip with his therapy as much as possible before I had to leave. He had worked very hard and accomplished a good deal. He could get in and out of his chair with very little help and was able to move his arms through a much broader range than before. Mauricia, of course, was horrified. Forever hostile toward me, she moaned and groaned and complained about practically everything. I ignored her. I was determined to help Skip, particularly as his nurse was encourag-

ing me and seemed very pleased about the influence I was
having on the boy.

James had formed the habit of eating as many meals as
he could with Skip in his room. And he seemed to have
reverted to the indifference toward me he'd shown when I
first arrived. It wasn't important since I saw very little of
him—just enough to say hello when we ran into each other
infrequently in the hallways or Skip's room.

On one occasion, I nervously stopped him in the hall.
"Do you think it would be all right for me to write a
letter?" I asked abruptly.

He looked at me in surprise. "A letter?"

"Yes. To New York . . . ."

"You mean you want to get in touch with your husband?
Come to think of it, that might not be such a bad idea," he
said bitterly.

"Not my husband," I said quickly. "I have a friend I
promised to keep in touch with. I'd like to write to her."

"Of course. You're not in jail, you know," he replied
easily. "There's a box in the village. If you write your letter
and drop it in the box, the mailman will pick it up. You can
buy postage at the tobacco exchange."

I'll write to Sandra, I thought to myself. *I know I can
trust her.*

It was quite evident that as the days went by and Martin
did nothing to locate me, I was becoming of less and less
importance. But I couldn't be sure James was not above
holding Martin's indifference against me, personally blam-
ing this unexpected turn of events on me and turning the
hostility he had been nurturing against my husband in my
direction.

I couldn't help but notice how very different the two
brothers were. They were so much alike physically, and

yet in character they seemed worlds apart. Even making allowances for James's personality having changed drastically for the worse since the death of his wife, he was not the open, loving person Michael was.

Twelve days after my interlude on the deserted island with Michael, I finally received a reply from Sandra. She said that Martin had let it be known I had disappeared and was intending to use the note I had left him as grounds for divorce. It would allow him to remarry, and the likely candidate for his fourth wife was the beautiful, voluptuous Sylvia.

Of course, the whole thing is being carried out very discreetly. Martin is much too proud to let anyone know that his wife walked out on him. And his army of lawyers will take full advantage of the situation. Be sure they'll be able to find a way for him to save face no matter what.

Sandra's news left me quite indifferent. Somehow, I seemed to have nothing in common with those people anymore. My previous way of life had disappeared, as though in a haze. The life I had lived with Martin, with little or no enthusiasm, was a life lived by someone else. It seemed as though I had not begun to live at all until coming to the island. Although I wasn't free, at least I wasn't someone else's puppet. Ironically, here I had become my own person. The island had done wonders for me. The truth was, I didn't want to leave it.

Sandra had made no mention of my address, nor did she ask how I had come to be where I was. She must have been asking herself many questions, but if nothing else, she knew when to be discreet. She had closed her letter by offering me her help, however, were I to find that I needed it, and I was very moved by her consideration.

Undoubtedly she was assuming that I had found a job, since she did mention something about my work, adding that I was to be admired for being so practical about everything.

> If you've found a good job, hang on to it. Being naive, you've put yourself in a rather bad light in this separation from Martin and you can be very sure that he'll do whatever needs doing to make you look even worse. Your note, the fact that you took off without a word to anyone in the midst of one of the most important social events of the season—it all adds up to Martin holding a very strong hand. He'll use every single thing he can think of without the slightest regard for you or your feelings. And don't think for a minute that you can expect to get any alimony from him.

I laughed at the very thought of getting alimony from Martin. I didn't want alimony or anything else from him. I had severed all the ropes that had tied me to him and had set out for the open sea.

THERE WAS ONE THING, however, that I had to do before I left the island. My ring was still with the shopkeeper. It didn't mean anything to me emotionally, but it was worth quite a bit and I couldn't just throw it away. Not wanting to bother anyone else about it, I set out on foot late the next morning and headed for the village. And I had the good sense to put on one of the white, wide-brimmed hats so common on the island to protect my head against the hot sun.

It felt wonderful to be walking, free and alone, unrecognized as I made my way through the countryside. The road wound through the profusion of green vegetation and tropical flowers. The leaves on the trees reflected the bright sunlight and the long vines seemed almost amorous in the way they clung to the tree trunks. The fruit of the bread trees hung down between the leaves, looking like giant potatoes. Here and there I could see the red-tiled roof of a worker's house sparkling in the sun amid the green vegetation.

Along the way I met several of the charming native women coming home from the market, their baskets balanced on their heads and their arms filled with bundles. They were laughing and talking as they walked, looking very attractive in their customary lace blouses and colorful skirts.

They smiled greetings to me as they passed, their faces warm and friendly. They seemed full of the joy of life, and walked with exquisite grace, their flowing skirts swaying in rhythm with their steps. As they went on their way, I could hear their voices raised in song.

Where the roadway took me close enough to one of the small houses, a woman would appear in the doorway and invite me to come in. Anxious to reach the village, I had to refuse, but I did stop to talk for a moment.

"Where are you from?" I was asked invariably.

"From New York," I replied.

"New York, America?"

"Yes, New York!" I laughed.

They marveled at the thought that I was from New York, and I could see a thousand questions in their eyes.

"I've never been to New York," said one woman wistfully.

I was struck by the perversity of human nature. Those women dreamed of living in New York, while I envied them their life of serenity in an island paradise. Little did they know that I would gladly have traded the tensions and frustrations of city living for their life among the tropical flowers and banana trees!

To be able to live there, with the man I would choose to be my husband. . . . To live without worry or fear, without all the problems and artificialities, just to enjoy living, day after day. . . .

I continued my dreaming as I went on with my solitary walk to the village. To get to the small shop I had to cross the marketplace, which was just about to close. The butchers were taking in their meats and fish peddlers were packing in ice the few fish they had left, for nothing could be left out for very long in the heat. The ground was littered with discarded fruits and vegetables.

In the open areas a few determined vendors remained. They were offering everything from scarves to nutmeg to vanilla, coconuts, fruit, vegetables. . . . And whatever was left was being sold at rock-bottom prices. Although I was sorely tempted, I managed to resist.

When I finally spoke to the shopkeeper, I discovered he had sold my ring to one of the engineer's wives. He quickly gave me the money for it.

Coming out of the shop, I noticed Michael's Land Rover going by. Suddenly shy, I started to duck back into the doorway but he had already seen me. He backed up and stopped next to me.

"Finished your shopping?" he asked with a smile, his blue eyes sparkling, his handsome face tanned. So, I thought to myself, he was as handsome as I had remembered. . .and as charming. It hadn't been a fantasy.

"Uh, yes. . .thanks. You're back!" I stammered, unable to keep the pleasure out of my voice.

"Yes. I returned last night." He looked up at the sky where clouds had begun to gather on the ocean side. "Looks like it might rain," he said.

"Rain! With the sun the way it is?"

"Here, the sun can be shining one minute and the rain coming down in buckets the next. Especially this time of the year. Thunderstorms come and go in no time at all, but you can get soaked in a few seconds. Let me drive you back to the house."

"Will I be taking you out of your way?" I asked.

"Not really. But if you don't mind, I'd like to drop in at the banana warehouse on the way."

The prospect pleased me very much. I climbed into the car and we headed toward the north end of the island. As we drove along, the storm burst and I was very happy to be in the shelter of the car.

"You certainly came along at the right time," I said with satisfaction.

"It won't last. Look, the sky's beginning to clear even now."

Looking out over the sea, I could see that the sky was clear and blue. The rain had stopped as suddenly as it had started.

"My guess is that you haven't had lunch yet," suggested my companion, and I had to agree with him.

"Then we'll eat at the banana plant," he said.

I was delighted with my good fortune at this chance meeting. "Lucky for me you came by," I repeated like a star-struck schoolgirl.

"Just as lucky for me," he replied. "I'm glad I was able to help." His eyes told me he was feeling more than his words said.

After a moment, he asked curiously, "Do you go to that shop very often?"

"Oh, no! This is only my second time. I was there once before, with Christine."

He made no comment and I continued. "He has all sorts of lovely things there. I bought some material and made myself a couple of dresses. . . ."

"Good for you! You seem to have many skills."

"Well, I had to find something to do with my time," I sighed. "And they'll be part of my memories."

"Hmmm. . . . Memories of a very bad time, I expect," he said, grimacing.

I didn't pick up on his remark. Nothing had been said about my leaving since our talk on the deserted island.

The road wound up the side of the hill and as we climbed, the scenery changed. Michael turned onto a side road that had been cut through thick vegetation that almost blocked out the sun.

"It's like a jungle!" I exclaimed.

"Don't be afraid," he said in a calm voice. "I'm taking this road because I wanted you to see something. It won't take long to get there."

In the distance I could hear the sound of chopping. It seemed to be coming from the depths of the forest.

"That sound is made by one of the woodcutters," explained Michael, seeing my curiosity. "My ancestors must all have started out as woodcutters. It took a lot of courage and hard work to clear this wild land and plant the first banana trees."

The forest finally gave way to cultivated fields. As far as the eye could see were rows of banana trees.

The Land Rover came to a stop in front of some houses that were grouped around what appeared to be an old tower with a brass-covered roof. As soon as Michael got out of the car he was surrounded by men, women and children, all trying to talk at once. It was obvious that Michael was very popular with them and each tried to get close enough to touch him, shake his hand, ask him questions. With infinite patience, Michael tried to answer them all, speaking in Creole.

"They're quite excited," he said as he turned to me. "They tell me they saw the zombie last night and that means the volcano is going to erupt very shortly."

"What's the zombie?" I asked.

"A strange creature that's part of the Caribbean folklore. I guess you could call it a ghost. At any rate, it's supposed to be able to come back from the dead with news of impending disaster. What it does is scare the living! They are very impressed by these things. Who knows. . .there may be truth in these old legends. Or perhaps the wind rattled a few doors last night, or blew some of the branches from the trees. Either way, it would have been enough to convince these people that the zombie had paid a visit. What with smoke from the volcano being much heavier than usual, they're terrified!"

We went into the tower, which served as an office and reception area. There were several rooms, in the walls of which were very narrow openings to let in the light.

As we were looking around, a young girl appeared, dressed in native costume. Her eyes were large and clear with thick lashes. She was dark skinned and wore a hibiscus blossom in her jet black hair. I was speechless, awed by her natural beauty.

Seeing Michael, the girl let out a small cry of joy and ran to him, flinging her arms around his neck. I could almost see her heart pounding, the neckline of her dress was so low.

He put his arms around her waist and pulled her close to him as he kissed her. I wanted to run. Witnessing this spectacle was quite unbearable. Realizing, to my chagrin, that I was jealous, I turned away, pretending to be fascinated by the posters on the wall. Then I heard Michael's voice.

"Vivian, come and meet Flora. I'm her godfather. I've known her from the minute she was born and I adored her!"

Behind the girl, a handsome young man came into the room.

"And this is Ernest," continue Michael. "Her fiancé. The two of them run this place."

I felt as though I had suddenly been relieved of a heavy burden. In my heart, however, I was anything but proud of the reaction I had had.

The two young people were very friendly. As soon as they heard we hadn't had our lunch, they dashed around preparing something for us to eat.

In no time we were all sitting on the terrace around a table laden with refreshments. The beautiful Creole girl poured rum and cane syrup over ice cubes, added lime juice and a small slice of lime. Her movements were gentle and very graceful, and whenever she spoke her voice was soft and warm and very kind.

Flora went out to prepare something further and Ernest stood talking quietly to Michael about the problems on the plantation.

I looked around me and my eyes came to rest on the

mysterious mountain with its billowing smoke. All around it the sky was very blue. In the peace of the day, the volcano appeared to be quite inoffensive.

"I've been trying to make you a typical Creole lunch," announced Flora. I was a little startled at the sound of her voice so close to me. I hadn't seen her come back. "Very Creole, in fact," she went on. "Avocado, gumbo, cabbage, hearts of palm...."

Nor was that all. We also had broiled lobster and then a delicious fruit salad.

After lunch, Michael showed me around the plant. I was surprised to see that coffee and a great variety of apples were grown there, in addition to bananas. Michael cautioned me about the manchineel tree, which he warned was very dangerous.

"It's known as the killer tree," he explained.

"I've heard about that," I said. "But I thought it was all just hearsay."

"It isn't just legend, unfortunately. Don't get too close to it—the sap is extremely corrosive. Even rain dripping from its branches can be enough to cause a burn. And don't ever sit under a manchineel tree, either. The little apples that fall from it are also very toxic. It's said that the men who sailed with Christopher Columbus who ate its fruit subsequently died."

"Good Lord! I wouldn't want a poisonous tree like that in my garden!" I exclaimed. "Thanks for the warning."

He smiled. "It won't be long before you know all the island's secrets," he said.

Just in time to leave it, I thought to myself sadly.

It was getting late, and after discussing a few more details with Ernest, Michael decided it was time for us to go. In the car, he handed me a small carton. "For you," he said simply.

Intrigued, I examined the outside of the box. "What is it?" I asked eagerly.

"Open it and see."

I opened the carton. Then I looked up at Michael, my eyes blinking. I felt confused and embarrassed. And I could see the troubled look in my companion's eyes. "Why?" I murmured.

At the bottom of the box in a bed of cotton batting lay my wedding ring, which I had sold to the shopkeeper.

"It's yours, isn't it?" said Michael in a dry voice.

"But I sold it!" I replied.

"And I bought it!" he retorted. "So that I could give it back to you."

"I don't understand," I mumbled, thoroughly confused.

"We can't have you selling your wedding ring!" he asserted.

"But it's mine!" I protested. "I can do whatever I want with it!"

"Not here, you can't. Not sell it, at any rate. Not on this island. You were brought here against your will and had no time to gather up even the necessities. . .like money, for instance. The shopkeeper paid you much less than it's really worth. No, Vivian, that's your wedding ring and you're to keep it!"

"But the man paid me for it!" I cried. "I insist on giving the money to you!"

"No, you won't. It's just part of the overall expense of this ridiculous operation," he replied in a wry tone.

For several minutes neither of us said a word. I could feel the tension between us. I could tell by his tone that any further protest on my part would only make him angry.

"How did you find out?" I asked in a small voice.

"It wasn't difficult. I often go into that shop to pick up something for the house. I saw the ring in the glass case and I knew it was yours; I had noticed it on you the night you were brought here. I asked the shopkeeper about it and he told me your story. I didn't want him selling it to anyone else." Then he added, "I had just picked it up. We almost ran into each other in the shop."

I was feeling more and more embarrassed. And my emotions, to say the least, were mixed. My face was burning and I was quite sure it must have been as red as the hibiscus flower in Flora's hair.

"What's wrong?" he asked after a moment of embarrassed silence. "What's bothering you?"

"That you had to pay for this ring, I guess...when I'd already been given money for it."

"Let's just say it's a gift from my brother and me. A small enough compensation for all the aggravation you've had to suffer." He spoke with tenderness in his voice.

"But, I...."

"Please, let's just forget the whole thing," he interrupted, his tone leaving no room for reply.

Chapter 13

It was time for me to start really thinking about leaving. But even though Michael had offered to take me back to New York, I simply couldn't seem to make up my mind. The same old problems would be waiting for me there. In fact, they were already beginning to bother me. My suitcases had been at the railway station all this time; I'd have to pick them up. And there were any number of other matters to be settled. I'd have to find out exactly where I stood, look for a job, find a place to stay.... No wonder I was procrastinating! Life on the island was so calm, so peaceful...so beautiful.

The day Michael came back, I was to have dinner with the two brothers in the dining room for the first time since he had left.

That afternoon, Christine told me that James was in a foul humor, shouting at everyone in the household and even creating something of a panic among the workers in the field. Christine's husband, it seemed, had also been subjected to his bad temper. I thought of what Michael had said about James, and I felt alarmed. What if he became uncontrollable? What might he do?

"Thank heaven Michael is back," Christine added. "Maybe he'll be able to calm him down."

Silently, I agreed.

WE SAT DOWN TO DINNER in an atmosphere that was oppressively heavy. Michael was trying to relieve the tension by telling us some of the funny things that had happened to him on his trip. But James wasn't listening; he seemed concerned about only one thing. Finally, he started to talk about it.

"I've come to a decision," he said, turning to me, his face steely with hate. "Since your husband doesn't seem to want to do anything, I'm going to force him to make a move."

I started to tremble, wondering what on earth he might have in mind. He was glaring at me belligerently.

"I'm going to write to him and tell him that you're here and will be kept here until he's willing to negotiate your release and do whatever he has to do to guarantee your freedom—and safety," he added ominously. "Furthermore, I intend to send a copy of my letter to every newspaper, radio station, television station and magazine in New York. It will have to come out in public. This time there'll be no escape for Martin Fawkes, no matter how powerful he may think he is, nor how influential his friends may be!"

He emphasized his words by striking the table with his fist, shaking the dishes and glassware, his lips drawn and taut, his eyes gleaming fanatically.

Michael and I looked at each other. I was stunned. I didn't want that kind of scandal. I knew what Martin's reaction would be. We'd all be in trouble.

Now I saw what Michael had been talking about. James was insane! And yet he seemed quite determined to see his plan through. There didn't seem to be any way to stop him. Except, perhaps, one.... No matter what, he had to be persuaded to change his mind.

After dinner, I found Michael on the veranda. James had gone upstairs to see his son.

I waited until after Henry had served the after-dinner coffee and brandy before approaching him. "Michael?" I ventured timidly. He seemed lost in thought.

Finally he turned around slowly, and when he spoke his voice was calm. "I know what you're going to say. My brother is out of his mind and won't listen to reason. He's jumpier than he's ever been; he seems to have reached the end of his rope. And he won't give up until he's dropped his little bomb. It's all uncontrollable madness with him, I'm afraid. I don't know what to do, save having him institutionalized."

"Wouldn't it help if I leave?" I asked.

He leaned back against the railing and looked at me thoughtfully. "It does seem like the only solution, doesn't it? If you're not here, then he won't have a hostage. And without a hostage, he can't carry out his plan."

"I'll leave right away, before he has a chance to do anything."

Michael spoke as if he were thinking out loud. "He'll be getting his letter off tomorrow," he said. "I know him. When he gets an idea stuck in his mind, he doesn't waste any time."

He was silent for a moment, thinking, before continuing. "You'll have to go before he can send that letter," he said finally.

"Your offer to help me...is it still good?" I asked anxiously.

"Of course," he said quickly. "My brother was the one who brought you here and I'll be the one who takes you home," he laughed ruefully. "I'm going to miss you, you know," he added in a warm voice.

When I looked at him I saw that his eyes were sad. "And I'm going to miss everything about this island," I replied.

"Are you serious?" he asked, his blue eyes searching my face.

"Very," I replied quickly. "You've been very kind to me while I've been here."

"I'm happy to hear it," he said quietly.

And then we both stopped talking, as though there was nothing else we had to say to each other. There seemed to be something caught in my throat and I was afraid I was going to cry. I felt like a fool.

I moved quickly to the table to pour the coffee and brought him back a cup. We drank slowly and I looked beyond the railing at the magnificent scenery bathed in the blue haze of evening. Was it possible that tomorrow this gorgeous horizon would be far behind me, becoming dim and obscure with the passing of time?

And what about the motionless figure, silent and tall, standing beside me? The symbol of something precious I had never known before, something I didn't even dare admit to myself....

Michael put down his cup and once again leaned back against the railing, his face turned up to the night sky. The air was filled with the soft, wild scents of the natural beauty stretched out before us.

Why did I have to leave? Why did I have to tear myself away from this dreamworld, this world that I was just beginning to discover?

I found myself reacting to a desperate impulse. Stepping close to Michael, I put my hand on his arm and forced him to look at me. "Michael...."

"Yes," he said quietly.

"Oh, Michael...." My voice was pleading.

He knew. He was not surprised. He simply reached out and put his arms around me and held me very close. I didn't know whether to laugh or cry. I had never felt such happiness...nor had I ever felt such pain.

For a long time we stood like that, just holding each other. Neither of us seemed able to move away.

Why was I leaving? Why couldn't I stay here, close to Michael, listening to his heartbeat in rhythm with my own, stay here and simply let myself be swallowed up by the immense joy I was feeling?

But there was still James. And there was still his wife's death. The death that had been caused by my husband. All of this remained to drive us apart.

Suddenly, Michael's voice echoed through the night. "I'll have to fly you out in the morning," he said. "We'll leave at eight o'clock. We should be in New York by late afternoon. You can go back to your husband, to your life, and forget all of this, Vivian...."

Forget? Did he really think it would be so easy? I turned and ran, my throat full of tears. I hurried to my room and sadly got out the small suitcase I had bought from the shopkeeper. I started to pack the few things that belonged to me. The small items I had purchased at the local market seemed very precious, even the dresses I had made myself from the material I'd bought.

Lucille had come to my room and was keeping me company. We had developed a friendship since our unpromising beginning. I was going to miss her.

For a while, I had been hearing a low rumbling sound that I thought must have been caused by a low-flying plane or a storm in the distance. When I looked at Lucille, I saw she had stopped folding the dress she held in her hands and was standing quite motionless, her face reflecting fear. Head to one side, she seemed to be listening for something.

Dropping the dress into the suitcase, she turned and walked to the window. Intrigued, I joined her. The blue haze I had noticed over the island before had become much thicker and was now gray, as though filled with fine dust.

"What is it?" I asked. "Fog?"

Lucille shook her head and only looked at me with frightened eyes.

At that moment, our attention was brought back to the inside of the room by a sudden noise. It was the crystal chandelier swaying from side to side, as though blowing in a strong wind. But there was no wind in the room!

Then we both jumped at a sudden crash. One of the pictures had fallen off a wall.

"The Tilsun!" Lucille exclaimed as she rushed toward the door. "The volcano! It's the volcano!" She ran down the hall, warning everyone in the house.

I ran after her. Pandemonium had broken loose. Servants, clutching their children by the hand, seemed to be running in all directions. Everyone was yelling directions at everyone else. The rumbling noise was becoming louder and louder.

Michael came into the hallway and stood beside me. He was calm in the midst of the confusion, but his face showed signs of concern. "Don't be afraid," he said quietly. "You aren't in any danger here. Of course, we'll have to postpone your flight out."

"It *is* dangerous, isn't it?" I ventured timidly.

"You mean the volcano might erupt? Well, that's always a possibility. But the village has to be evacuated—at least the part that would be in danger if the volcano should go up. I've already begun to organize the evacuation."

"Is there anything I can do?" I asked.

He walked away quickly without answering and I heard the Land Rover start up and drive away into the distance. I went out onto the balcony. The air was filled with fine dust. I looked toward the mountain and saw sparks flashing in the smoke billowing from the Tilsun. The air surrounding it was shimmering and the earth trembled below.

Lights could be seen moving around everywhere in the night as people rushed to the endangered area. Everyone on the island seemed to accept responsibility for the safety of others.

I ran to Skip's room and was met by Mauricia at the door. "He's okay, I'm looking after him. Don't worry," she whispered.

With that off my mind, I went to join the others. Christine was giving orders, but everyone seemed to be in a panic and there was nothing but confusion.

"Get the rooms ready," she said to one of the servants. "They're going to have to evacuate the school and the orphanage, and the children won't have any place to go. We'll have to take them in here." After assigning duties to the others, Christine ran to the garage and backed out the truck.

I quickly ran to her. "Where are you going?" I asked.

"They'll be needing all the help they can get with the

evacuation." she replied. "There are people living in all those houses. I'm going to see what I can do."

"Take me with you," I pleaded.

She looked at me and shook her head. "It's too dangerous. It looks as if there's going to be an eruption, and when the lava starts flowing...."

"So? It's dangerous for you, too, isn't it?" I replied tartly.

"Yes, but I'm part of the plantation. You aren't."

"What difference does that make? I want to help. Please, Christine, I want to go with you."

She hesitated, but before she could say anything more, I was in the truck. "All right," she said simply.

It was quite a trip. The volcano kept on rumbling and particles of soot flew through the air and stuck to our skin. The air was thick with dust. As we drew closer to the volcano we could see the fire: it was terrifying. From time to time there would be a small explosion and Christine would stop the truck. As the explosion died down, we would start off again.

"What scares me most," confessed Christine, "are the rocks being hurled from the volcano. The road could be cut off."

I could sense the tension in her, but she was managing to maintain an outward appearance of calm.

I was very worried. Where was Michael? Where was James? What was going to happen? This was a catastrophe for which we had not been prepared.

The tropical night was fast losing its charm. The air had become quite oppressive and everywhere there was the taste of ashes. No longer magic in its silence, the night was filled with sudden sounds, terrifying and mysterious. In a very few hours, paradise had become transformed into a hell.

When we reached the village on the slope of the mountain beneath the volcano, I began to feel as though I were being hurled into a nightmare. It was chaos. People were running back and forth, some trying to drag their animals behind them. Every kind of vehicle had been assembled to help evacuate the people.

What appeared to be an endless line of people, most of whom were carrying great bundles on their heads, moved along the road. The heat was suffocating and there was a strong odor of sulfur in the air. The atmosphere alternated between black and red.

Shadows scurried frantically back and forth in front of the bungalows, and voices could be heard coming from every direction. Throughout all the confusion, explosion after explosion sporadically occurred.

Suddenly I heard Michael's voice coming through a loudspeaker. "Don't panic! We have no reason to believe that there'll be an eruption! To be out of danger, however, everyone must be away from the side of the mountain. Do not try to take your belongings with you—there isn't time! Safety first! Leave at once. Take only the essentials! Remember, the important thing is to get out safely! Everyone, leave quickly."

And from another direction came the sound of James's hysterical voice calling through a loudspeaker. "Hurry along. Keep moving! Don't block the road!" His voice was tense and shrill.

Christine and I had come upon a group of children and were taking them to the truck. Busy as I was, I could still hear the ominous rumblings of the volcano and feel the trembling of the earth under my feet. I couldn't help thinking of the things I had read about volcanoes—how entire towns and cities had been wiped out by their eruptions. Would such a thing happen here?

Smoke continued to billow from the mouth of the volcano. The tension of not knowing what would happen was becoming unbearable.

The children safely in the truck, I started back toward the school for one last check for more children, only to run headlong into the figure of a man in the darkness.

"What are you doing here?" a voice exclaimed in surprise.

At the sound of his voice I was reassured. It was Michael. "I came with Christine to help with the children."

"It's not safe here. You must go back to the house!" he said urgently, shouting over the roar in the background. "Can't you see...I'm responsible for you. You're taking a terrible risk, coming here. Please, Vivian, go home."

Suddenly I felt sick. My mind was horrified at the thought that the whole island might explode, and fear filled my heart. I groaned.

"What is it?" asked Michael, alarmed.

"I'm afraid," I said simply, hanging my head.

He put his arm around my shoulders. "Vivian...you never should have come here."

I couldn't control my trembling and clung to him in a kind of desperation. "I'm afraid I'm not very brave," I mumbled. "But I'll be all right in a minute. I have to help Christine with the children."

I felt his soft lips against my cheek. He smelled of smoke and sulfur, and my hands clinging to his vest could feel the dust and soot that covered him from head to foot. I didn't care. It was an incredible joy to be so close to him. And then his lips touched mine and for a second the world around us disappeared.

He pulled away from me. "Vivian! We must be mad! For God's sake, go back to the house with Christine! Look after Skip; he needs you. Promise that you will?"

I nodded my consent.

"I must go. There's so much to do. It will be a long night." He kissed me gently, turned and hurried away. I watched him go, growing smaller and smaller as the distance between us lengthened, until there was nothing to see but the night and the sporadic flashes of red.

My attack of fear seemed to have passed and I was able to move ahead on legs that were again steady. I checked the houses one last time. In one hut I found a child hiding in fright under a sheet on a bed. Gently I coaxed the terrified and sobbing girl into my arms and started back to the truck.

Christine was looking for me. "We're ready to go! The truck is full. We're taking the children and one nun back to the house."

"What about the others? I'm sure there are more."

"They're being taken to the hospital. We'll know tomorrow if there are any serious problems."

After the spectacle we had just witnessed and the hours we had just survived, the calm of the house seemed like a miracle. But there was no time to think. We had the children to look after. Henry had prepared lots of food and punch and we left the children to the supervision of Sister Rose Marie. Beds had been made ready for them all.

When everyone had been settled, Christine came to me. Her hair was a mess and her face was black from the smoke. I knew I must look the same. Her lips were pale with fatigue, but she wasn't giving up. I had to admire her.

"If you want my advice," she said in a voice husky from exhaustion, "you'll try to get some sleep. You may be needed tomorrow."

I had no idea how much she knew about my personal problems in the midst of this larger crisis, but she leaned forward to give me a great hug. I felt much better for this gesture of friendship and promised to take her advice.

But first I went to Skip's room. Fortunately, he and Mauricia were both sound asleep. Skip seemed to be quite unaware of what was going on all around them. Reassured, I retired to my room.

Over the ocean, a new dawn was breaking. The sky was still dark with the dust. Life would go on, it seemed, despite the tragedy on the mountain. I washed as much of the soot off as I could. There was so much it seemed it would be part of me forever. Feeling strangely sad, I got into bed, totally exhausted. My last thought was of Michael, wondering if he was safe. But sleep claimed me almost immediately.

Chapter 14

It was late the next morning when I awoke, my mind and body still suffering fatigue. I got out of bed and went to the window. The sun was shining dimly through a haze of dust on a blackened landscape. I looked at the mountain and saw that smoke and vapor were still billowing from it, but the situation did not seem to have worsened.

Beneath my window, a group of children played around Skip's wheelchair close to the swimming pool. The fine coat of dust and soot everywhere delighted them as in a game. They had just survived a catastrophe, yet seemed quite unaware of it.

Somewhat reassured, I dressed quickly and went downstairs. Christine greeted me on the veranda. She must have given herself a thorough scrubbing, because she was immaculate, her blond hair shining in the sunlight.

"The volcano seems to have settled down," I said hopefully.

"For the moment, maybe," she said curtly.

"You're pessimistic!" I accused her.

"Who knows?" she shrugged. "These things are always unpredictable. They tell me the last eruption occurred some fifteen years ago. Since then it's been completely quiet. Then, all of a sudden...." She threw up her hands in an explosive gesture.

I asked her about the children.

"Precisely," she replied, somewhat ambiguously, as she sat down and poured a cup of coffee. "I'm very worried about them. I don't know whether we'll be keeping them here for a while or whether they'll be sent to another school until they can go back to their own."

"Couldn't James or Michael tell you anything?" I asked.

She looked at me and frowned. "I haven't seen them. Neither one has returned since last night."

"They must be busy finding shelter for all the people who had to be evacuated."

"Yes," she sighed. "Meanwhile, I've arranged to have a meal prepared for the children."

She turned to look at the mountain. At that distance, scarcely any of the damage could be seen. The volcano seemed much less active.

Suddenly, Christine turned to speak to me. "Would you like to take a trip to the village?" she proposed.

"Do you think they might need help?" I asked.

"I don't know," she replied. "I don't imagine so, now that the evacuation is over. But we can find out easily enough. We'll drive carefully."

"Okay," I agreed.

We got into the old truck and started off down the same road we had taken the previous night. The closer we got to the village, the more smoke and soot filled the air. When we got to the edge of the settlement we could see the thick layer of ash covering the streets and houses all the way up the side of the mountain.

There was no sign of life. The people and animals had all fled. The houses and stables were empty, their doors swinging sadly in the breeze.

"Where is everyone?" I asked Christine.

"They've been housed temporarily in several buildings around the plantation for the most part. Some are in tents and some have been taken in by other people."

"What about food? Good heavens, it's going to be a problem feeding them all!" I exclaimed in consternation.

"Oh, I'm sure Michael has done whatever was necessary to take care of it. He got all the workers together and gave them all jobs to do. My husband must have been one of them. I haven't seen him since last night."

We didn't meet a soul throughout the entire trip. The village was like a ghost town. As we were going back to the house, we heard the bells of the church. It was a mournful sound.

I had a feeling of dreadful foreboding. We finished the drive in silence, my heart breaking to see the once bright tropical landscape blackened and burdened with soot. The vegetation was now dying. I wondered if much of it would be able to recover.

I knew the moment I saw Henry running out to the truck from the house that my presentiment had proven to be true.

"Henry, what is it?" Christine called out in alarm.

"Mr. deVergoff...he...." Henry held his face in his hands.

My heart stopped. I started trembling, fearing the worst.

"Henry, please, go on..." Christine implored.

He looked at her, his eyes sunken in his haggard face. "There was an accident," he muttered. "Doctor Michael...."

"No!" I cried out softly, the tears streaming down my cheeks. "It can't be true," I whispered to myself.

"Go on," Christine encouraged him, her arm around me for comfort and strength. "Tell us."

"Doctor Michael...he says that Mr. deVergoff is dead."

The last word hung in the air like a thick, black cloud.

"James? Oh, no!" Christine exclaimed. "It can't be true!"

I bowed my head, weak with both relief and grief, thankful with all my being that Michael was alive and well, and stunned by the news of James's death.

I looked up and saw Michael coming toward the truck from the house. I got out of the truck and ran to him.

"Michael, I'm...." But words were of little meaning. There was nothing I could say that would tell him what I was feeling. I reached my hands out to him, my face wet with tears. "I'm sorry," was all I could say, in a husky whisper, trying to hold back my tears.

He stood tall and angular against the blackened landscape, the still smoking volcano on the horizon behind him. Having worked all through the night and morning, he was still covered with the volcanic ash. His once white shirt was torn and covered with soot. His deep blue eyes expressed a tragic private sorrow.

"I understand," I said. He enveloped me in his arms and held me, mindless of Christine and Henry, mindless of the soot and the dirt. Nothing mattered at that moment but the comfort we could give each other.

In a husky, deep voice Michael gave me the details. "His car was found at the bottom of a ravine not far from the village. Probably he had gone back to the disaster area for one last check to make sure no one had been left behind. He had made several trips to move the villagers away from the danger area. He was working himself right into the ground.

"He hadn't been himself for some time, as you know, and I guess the crisis last night was too much. He died of a heart attack. He died at the wheel of his car."

I could feel Michael's pain and wanted to share it. "Michael, is there anything I can do?" I offered.

"Yes, Vivian, there is. I hate to ask anything of you; you'll be going soon. But...it's about Skip...."

Skip! Poor little Skip. Once an orphan, crippled, and now orphaned again. How much could one little boy take? My heart broke at the thought of his sorrow. "Have you told...?"

"No, not yet, I won't...for a bit. But for now...could you stay with him and look after him? Until you go?"

"Go?" I queried tremulously, my eyes searching his face.

"Yes. There's no reason for you to stay here now. You should be back with your husband and friends, not here."

We stood in silence facing one another.

"I've arranged for someone to fly you to New York after the funeral tomorrow. I'm sorry, but I won't be able to go back with you, although I know I should. There's so much to be done here."

He took my hand and kissed it. "I hope you'll find it in your heart to forgive James someday," he said quietly. "He was a tormented, driven soul."

Before I had time to say a word, he drew me to him and kissed me tenderly. "Goodbye," he said, and jumped into his Land Rover and drove off.

THAT SAME NIGHT, James's body was brought back to the house. All of the people living on the island came to pay their respects. Tears of sorrow coursed down their faces, black and white alike. James deVergoff had been more than respected; he had earned the affection of these people by administering the affairs of the island to their best interests, and they knew it.

An aged storyteller came, as was the custom, and related the virtues and boasted the merits of the deceased.

And as though the forces of nature considered the life of the lord of the island sufficient sacrifice, the horizon over the mountain cleared gradually until eventualy there was no sign of volcanic activity at all. One could only hope that the peace and quiet would be permanent and that life on the island would return to normal.

James was buried the next day. A long procession followed the casket to the cemetery. There were flowers everywhere. On the simple wooden cross bearing the name of Catherine deVergoff, a second name had been inscribed. James deVergoff had joined the wife he had loved so much.

I added my bouquet of flowers to those of the other mourners and went back to the house, filled with sadness.

During that day I had not seen the man who was now sole master of St. Victor Island. Michael had been acting as host, greeting all the people who had come to pay their respects, looking after everything himself. I might have found the courage to offer my services, had there been an appropriate moment to speak to him. I had been spending most of my time with Skip and it was becoming more and more difficult to explain why the household was in such upheaval. Skip had been told that his father had been injured to explain why Mauricia and so many others had taken to weeping and sighing so often.

I was finding it very difficult trying to find a way to prepare the boy for the awful truth. I knew how much it would hurt him. Finally I decided to leave it for Michael to do; I simply didn't have the courage.

I was leaving in the evening.

Michael was in the study and his door was closed. The thought of leaving without seeing him once more was unbearable. It was all so ridiculous! At six o'clock, I would walk out of that house and out of his life. Forever.

I decided it would be worth the risk to see him again. My heart pounding in my ears, I strode purposefully to his door and knocked. I had twenty minutes before I had to get into the car that would take me to the landing strip. Twenty minutes in which to decide my fate.

"Come in!" called the voice I loved so much. I was in a panic.

I pushed the door open and saw him sitting behind the desk. *Oh, Michael,* I thought, *if only I could tell you how much I love you!*

"What is it?" he asked without looking up.

I resolutely walked across the room toward him. He raised his head.

"Vivian!" He stood quickly. "What are you doing here? I thought you'd left!"

He was staring at me, wide-eyed, as if he couldn't believe what he was seeing.

I stepped close to the desk. "The plane leaves in an hour."

He shook his head. "I would rather not have seen you," he said.

"There's something I want to show you, Michael, before I go," I stated.

"Vivian," he went on. "Your life is elsewhere. Please go. Go quickly. Forget all this."

I reached across the desk and put Sandra's letter down in front of him. "Read this. It will explain some things to you," I said simply.

He lowered his eyes to the paper and began to read. After finishing the letter, he then went back over part of it. Finally he lifted his head and frowned at me.

"Divorce? You...and your husband? What does it mean?"

He pushed back his chair as though to come around to the front of the desk where I was standing, but I put up my hand to stop him.

"Michael. I want to talk to you. It will only take a few minutes."

He nodded and sat down in his chair behind the desk. As he listened, his eyes darkened. When he finally spoke, it was in a vibrant voice. "Vivian! Does this mean that you and your husband are separated? That you're free?"

"Yes," I said simply. I was afraid to say more.

The silence between us tortured me. Why didn't he speak? In my heart I ached to stay...to live on this beautiful island with the man of my dreams forever. Here I had known the love and the happiness I thought I would never find...knew I would never find with another man.

But did he want me? I didn't dare express my feelings for fear of his refusal.

"Vivian," he finally ventured, breaking the silence.

As I leaned forward over the desk, my heart stopped. "Yes?" I asked breathlessly.

"My brother kidnapped you and brought you here by force. He tore you from your friends, your family—your world. Tore you suddenly, and abruptly. You and your husband are separated, true, but nevertheless New York is your home...."

No! I wanted to cry out. *New York is not my home. This island is my home, and you are my family.* But I waited, in fear.

"After what you've been put through by my brother, I know that what I'm about to ask is absurd. But...would you stay? Would you...live here, with us? We need you. Skips needs you...and I need you. There is so much that needs to be done...at the hospital, in the orphanage, in the village...." He paused and gazed at me with his open blue eyes.

I could no longer disguise my emotions. I returned his glance with all the love I was feeling. Yes! Yes! my heart was crying out in joy, but before I could speak, he jumped to his feet. In the next instant I felt his arms around me, strong and incredibly gentle.

"Vivian. It's true we need you here. But more important than that, I love you. I love you as I've never loved anyone before. More than I thought I ever could. I couldn't bear to let you go."

I burst into tears—tears of joy. Laughing and embarrassed, I brushed them away with the back of my hand.

"My darling!" Michael exclaimed. "What have I done?"

"No...it's not what you think," I laughed, returning his fervent kisses. "I'm crying for joy...because I love you, too, Michael. I couldn't live without you!"

"My prisoner," I heard him murmur, holding me in his arms. "My dear, precious prisoner.... You can't imagine how happy you're making me!"

Oh, but I did. I knew because I was feeling the same happiness. With all my heart and soul I had wanted this.

Dear Sandra, so much has happened since I last wrote. Michael and I were married very quietly, because of James's recent death, in St. Victor's Church, the oldest church in the Caribbean.

There is much ahead for both of us to do. Michael has a number of ideas for the betterment of working conditions for the people of the island while maintaining the unique character of the place.

The volcano is quiet now. It is calm and peaceful everywhere and the villagers have returned to their homes. Michael is hard at work on a plan that will guarantee their safety in the event of another eruption. It is designed to evacuate the village completely within minutes. If anyone can do it, I know Michael can.

We have a child, of course. Had him and loved him long before we were married. His name is Harold, but everyone calls him Skip. He was crippled in a car accident, but his condition is improving every day. Perhaps he finds hope in the knowledge that he is truly and dearly loved. Skip has always loved his Uncle Michael, and he is gradually learning to accept him as a devoted father.

As for me, I work with Michael in the hospital, learning from him, helping him . . . and loving him. All of the bitterness that had grown in me during my years in New York has completely disappeared. It is impossible to be bitter, even to remember bitterness, living in a tropical paradise with the man you love and who loves you.

Yes, I've found happiness. And, God willing, I'll be hanging on to it.

Everything you've always expected in a book!

Exciting novels of romance, suspense and drama, with intriguing characters and surprising plot twists, set against international backgrounds.

You will receive the newest in romantic suspense as soon as it's available!

As a Mystique subscriber you will automatically receive 4 new releases a month. Each novel is far more than you'd expect—even better than you could hope for. A whole new gallery of surprising characters in chilling and dramatic situations. A riveting entertainment experience . . . and for only $1.50 each.

House of Secrets by Denise Noël

As the prosecutor accused her of murder, Pascale remained silent. To defend herself demanded revealing a family secret that had been kept for eight long years. When she'd been hired by the wealthy Sévrier family she'd not expected terror and heartbreak . . . nor death!

Proper Age for Love by Claudette Jaunière

Anne didn't understand when her fiancé suggested she become his mistress, not his wife. She left him and steeled her heart against love forever. But her world was shattered years later by the sound of his voice. Fearing her heart might yet answer his call she fled . . . into a nightmare!

Island of Deceit by Alix André

Despite a threat to her life, Rosalie had to learn what had happened to her sister on the exotic Caribbean island of Sainte-Victoire. She soon found herself enmeshed in a web of intrigue . . . and in love with the one man she had most reason to fear.

High Wind in Brittany by Caroline Gayet

For weeks the tiny fishing village had been aflame with rumors about the mysterious stranger. Why had he come? What was he after? When Marie learned the truth she could not hold back her tears. She wept for him, for the townsfolk, but mostly . . . for herself.